"Oh, I've forgot. I have a letter for the earl."

Vivian spoke quite calmly as she addressed the handsomest man she had ever seen.

"If you leave it with the butler, I'm sure he'll give it to the earl." Reed paused, his gaze skimming over the out-of-fashion travel dress she wore, which was stained by the rigours of the trip from America. He could only assume she was the governess who accompanied the earl's granddaughter.

"You must be famished," he said now, kindly. "The butler will be glad to show you to the kitchen for a bite to eat." He smiled at her in a way that never failed to win favour among the servants in his own household and sauntered out the door.

Two spots of colour burned on Vivian's cheeks. She was the stepdaughter of Lady Pamela Spalding. Not some common serving wench.

"That gentleman who just left. What was his name?" she asked the butler.

"Do you mean Mr. Reed, miss? Mr. Lucian Reed?"

"Thank you," she said graciously. "I shall be sure to remember that."

Books by Clarice Peters

HARLEQUIN REGENCY ROMANCE
CONTRARY LOVERS
THE MARQUIS AND THE MISS
11–VANESSA
23–PRESCOTT'S LADY

Don't miss any of our special offers. Write to us at the following address for information on our newest releases.

Harlequin Reader Service
P.O. Box 1397, Buffalo, NY 14240
Canadian address: P.O. Box 603,
Fort Erie, Ont. L2A 5X3

THE HEART'S WAGER

CLARICE PETERS

Harlequin Books

TORONTO • NEW YORK • LONDON
AMSTERDAM • PARIS • SYDNEY • HAMBURG
STOCKHOLM • ATHENS • TOKYO • MILAN

Published July 1991

ISBN 0-373-31153-2

THE HEART'S WAGER

Copyright © 1991 by Laureen Kwock. All rights reserved. Except for use in any review, the reproduction or utilization of this work in whole or in part in any form by any electronic, mechanical or other means, now known or hereafter invented, including xerography, photocopying and recording, or in any information storage or retrieval system, is forbidden without the permission of the publisher, Harlequin Enterprises Limited, 225 Duncan Mill Road, Don Mills, Ontario, Canada M3B 3K9.

All the characters in this book have no existence outside the imagination of the author and have no relation whatsoever to anyone bearing the same name or names. They are not even distantly inspired by any individual known or unknown to the author, and all the incidents are pure invention.

The Harlequin trademarks, consisting of the words HARLEQUIN REGENCY ROMANCE and the portrayal of a Harlequin, are trademarks of Harlequin Enterprises Limited; the portrayal of a Harlequin is registered in the United States Patent and Trademark Office and in the Canada Trade Marks Office.

Printed in U.S.A.

CHAPTER ONE

"VISCOUNTS, EARLS, baronets... and what is the other—marquises? I vow, I shall never get them straight in my head!" Miss Aurora Spalding declared with a defiant shake of her guinea curls.

"Oh, but it's terribly easy really, Rory," her half sister, Vivian, replied. "Just concentrate. Let me explain it all again."

Agreeably enough, Rory listened to Vivian's melodic voice, which lulled her almost as much to sleep as the carriage carrying them from Bristol to London in this May of 1817.

"The most important thing to remember is that there is only one Prince," Vivian said, her wine-dark eyes compelling her sister to pay attention. "That's the Regent. His brothers are the royal dukes, then come the regular dukes, and after that the marquises, and the earls, and the viscounts, and the barons. Your grandfather is an earl, so you will have rank."

"But we are Americans, Viv. Americans believe in equality, not rank. Besides, Grandfather may be an earl but that doesn't make me an earless."

"Countess," Vivian corrected. "And you wouldn't be a countess. You would be..." Her heart-shaped face screwed up momentarily in a frown as she considered the situation. "It would all depend on whom you married."

"It's much easier being an American," Rory declared. "Why did Mother want to send us here to London, particularly when Grandfather doesn't even know we're coming?''

Vivian's murmured reply was lost in the carriage wheels' clattering over the rutted road. Rory sighed, yawned and settled her head once again on her sister's shoulder. Within minutes she was asleep. Vivian gazed at her fondly. With her upturned nose and her sweet smile curved in sleep, Rory resembled a soft tabby cat. She certainly looked much younger than her eighteen years. Vivian's brown eyes sobered as she pondered Rory's plaintive question just before she had fallen asleep. Vivian, for her part, knew only too well why her stepmother had dispatched them to London.

Lady Pamela Spalding, to give that lady her rightful name on her native soil, was a beautiful, spoiled young woman who had made a striking debut in Society. After one Season, several titled Englishmen dangled after her, but she had accepted an American, Thomas Spalding, who had taken her off to Philadelphia. Great was Lady Pamela's shock to discover that her American gentleman had a daughter by a first marriage. Motherhood ill became Lady Pamela. She was not cruel, but she was indifferent to a motherless child who might have warmed to a friendly hand.

When Rory was born, Vivian had rejoiced more than anyone in the household. Lady Pamela had been too exhausted by childbirth to take a hand in the babe's care, and her husband had been hoping for a son. So it was Viv who had doted on Rory and played with her.

And it was Viv, too, who had noticed, when Rory turned sixteen the previous year, that Lady Pamela was becoming envious of the compliments her daughter received. Vivian knew her stepmother was a beautiful, vain woman who would take seriously any rival for attention. To protect Rory, Vivian had set to work on their father, and by the end of a month's pleading had won his consent to send both Rory and herself to London to visit Rory's grandfather.

Lady Pamela Spalding had been an enthusiastic supporter to the idea.

Now, however, Vivian was beginning to have second thoughts about the plan, which had seemed so sensible back in Philadelphia. Her stepmother had always spoken of her father, the Earl of Atwater, as an ogre. Would he welcome two young American girls under his roof?

Rory yawned, and her head dug more heavily into Vivian's shoulder. Vivian felt her eyes closing, too. They would find out about his lordship, the ogre, soon enough, she was very sure. Until then they must gather their strength before bearding the lion in his den.

AN ATTACK OF GOUT WAS NOT a pleasant experience for anyone to endure, and the fourth Earl of Atwater was no exception. The earl, by nature a generous, benevolent employer, was apt to become a regular bear jaw, in the words of his valet, whenever the gout was running its course. He was prone to dismiss with impunity anyone who crossed his path.

At this moment the earl was seated in a gilded curricle chair in his drawingroom with his left foot propped in front of him, looking, as his butler remarked later to the other servants, deep in the sulks.

Such a comment would have infuriated the earl, since at the age of sixty-five one did not indulge in the sulks. Instead one brooded on the perilous tricks the body was prone to play on a man. He preferred to think of the gout as a trick of a malicious sprite, rather than as a consequence of his weakness for the Parisian sweets his chef presented to him daily.

Gloomily, he surveyed the empty room, taking no delight in the roaring fireplace, nor in the marble bust of Aristotle. There had been no warning that the gout was about to lay him low. Indeed, last night's dinner—the very last he would enjoy for a considerable time—had been superb: a capon roasted to perfection, three kinds of sweetmeats, and the pièce de résistance, the brandied pears. At the thought of the pears, his foot, swathed in a heavy bandage, twinged painfully.

"Blasted foot!" he exclaimed. All his plans would go by the board. He would be laid up for a week. He could neither ride nor walk without appearing the perfect buffoon. And it had happened today of all days, when he'd had every expectation of bidding for and winning a prize Arabian at the estate sale of an unlucky gamester.

Fortunately, last night at White's he had encountered Lucian Reed, who planned to attend the auction today. He had just dispatched a footman asking Reed to call in before going on to the sale, and he hoped to convince his distant cousin to enter a bid on the Arabian for him.

But even if he won it, would he be able to ride it? the earl wondered, glaring at his foot, which as though it could read his mind throbbed again, causing him to emit a groan of pain.

At the sound, the door to the room opened, and a tall silver-haired lady swooped in, carrying with her a tray of medications. The Earl of Atwater groaned again, this time in real trepidation.

Certainly the figure gliding towards him was not one which would strike terror in the hearts of many. Lady Edwina Farber, the earl's sister, was a kind-hearted woman of fifty-three years who had stood by Atwater during his wife's death years before, and whose own widowed state had induced her to accept a home in the earl's establishment. Unfortunately, Edwina was a notorious quack and determined to do battle with the gout. The earl closed his eyes now, debating which was worse to endure, the gout or Edwina's cures.

She had learned of his affliction a few hours ago and now would attempt to pour one or another foul-smelling concoctions down his throat. If he fended off her help he would then be obliged to listen to her scold him about his prodigious appetite for Parisian cooking.

"Does your foot still pain you?" she asked, bending over to examine his bandaged foot.

"No, not in the least," he lied manfully.

"Dissembler. If you consume a dozen lobster patties at every ball you are invited to—"

"Didn't eat a dozen at every ball," he protested, giving the bottle she picked up from the tray an uneasy look.

"Well, you certainly did at Lady Sefton's ball," Lady Edwina said.

The earl felt a spasm of guilt. By Jupiter, he should remind her that his rank dwarfed hers, but it probably didn't matter a jot to Edwina. She bullied him. Always had.

"And how many bottles of claret did you drink later at White's?" she quizzed.

"Only one. *Ow!*" he screamed as she gave his foot an absent-minded pat.

"I'm sorry," she said in dulcet tones, popping a spoonful of the odious medicine into his mouth.

He turned towards her in mute fury with the spoon stuck in his mouth. Forgetting his foot, he attempted to rise. This sparked a fresh outcry of pain. It was at that precise moment that the door opened, and Hardy, his butler, entered with Lucian Reed and someone who appeared to be Reed's current chère amie. The flaxen-haired creature took one look at the earl and burst into whoops of laughter.

The earl yanked the spoon out of his mouth and thrust it back at his sister.

"Reed, do you forget yourself?" he thundered.

The tall, dark-haired gentleman dressed in a coat of Bath blue superfine over biscuit pantaloons appeared undaunted by this greeting. He strolled in, bowing to Lady Edwina and turning a smile towards the earl.

"Actually, Charles, I fear it is you who has the abominably bad memory. You dispatched a footman asking me to call. Something about bidding on the Arabian at Fernrod's estate."

"Ah yes, but there was no necessity to bring *her* with you."

Reed followed the earl's august stare, which was pointed straight at the young lady still convulsed in giggles. She had retreated into a handkerchief, and Lady Edwina was offering her a glass of water. This merely sparked an attack of the hiccoughs, which a vigorous pounding of her back, also administered by Lady Edwina, did nothing to alleviate.

Reed's ready sense of the ridiculous rose to the fore. "I fear you have mistaken the matter," Reed replied, his upper lip twitching at the sight of the sorely afflicted young lady. She was much too young for his tastes, little more than a schoolroom miss, and the idea of him taking anyone so unfashionable under his patronage struck him to the core. Her curly blond hair was too long and fell every which way into her eyes, and she had on such a quiz of a dress.

Moreover, since he was practically betrothed to the most fashionable female in London, the very idea of a chère amie was out of the question, for Reed took matters of romance and ensuing marriage very seriously indeed.

"Then if she's not yours, who the devil is she?" the earl thundered.

Her attack of the giggles and hiccoughs now successfully laid to rest with the assistance of Lady Edwina, Miss Aurora Spalding was recalled to her manners.

"I am yours, my lord."

"*Mine?*" Atwater turned nearly apoplectic.

"Oh, I have put it badly, haven't I? Vivian would say that I have no manners, and she's been trying to school me in the carriage as to what I should do when I met you. Since you're an earl, I suppose I should curtsy, but I shan't be any good at that. And besides, Americans don't curtsy."

"They don't?" Lady Edwina asked in failing accents.

"No, they don't," Rory said firmly.

"Who is this female?" the earl demanded. "Reed, if this is one of your stupid jests, I am not in the mood for it. My foot pains me considerably. And who is this Vivian?"

"Should you like to meet her?" asked Rory. "She insisted that she would wait outside, since she is not, strictly speaking, family to you. But she is to me, so you do see that we are all connected!"

The earl looked wholly baffled. "Everyone in the ton knows you delight in jests of this sort, Reed. But it ain't funny."

"I believe the joke is one played on you by Lady Pamela Spalding," Mr. Reed replied.

The veins on the earl's neck stood out wildly. "What?"

The twinkle in Reed's blue eyes was very pronounced as he bowed to the earl. "Allow me to introduce you to your granddaughter, Miss Aurelia—"

"Aurora," Rory corrected.

"Aurora Spalding."

The effect of Reed's words was immediate. The earl paled and sank back against his chair. Lady Edwina, in her haste to thrust hartshorn against her brother's nose, jarred his foot, which brought a roar of protest from him again.

"Edwina, are you trying to kill me?" he asked.

"No, Charles, truly. I am so sorry. If you would only take this tonic."

Reed rose.

"Where are you going?"

"To bid on your Arabian, Charles," he replied. "Isn't that what you want me to do?"

"Yes, to be sure. Much obliged, Lucian."

With a smile and a bow to Lady Edwina and a wink at Rory, Reed sauntered out of the drawingroom, chuckling to himself.

Vivian, who had been waiting in the hallway, leapt to her feet when she caught sight of the smiling gentleman who had accompanied them up the stairs. She had no idea who he was, but his consequence must be enormous judging by the finery he wore and the air of command he assumed. He was also the handsomest man she had ever seen, with jet-black hair worn in a Brutus cut, piercing blue eyes, an aquiline nose and a very square jaw. Just gazing at him made her feel breathless.

"I thought I heard a cry," she said now, crossing the black-and-white marble lozenges which made up the floor. "Is Rory all right?"

Reed smiled, and Vivian found herself smiling back at once.

"She is fine. Charles was just a trifle overcome by his granddaughter's arrival."

"You call him Charles. But isn't the earl much older than you?"

"Yes, but he is my cousin, a very remote connexion, but a connexion nonetheless that allows me the freedom to address him by his Christian name."

"Oh, I've forgot. Her mother sent along a letter."

"If you leave it with Hardy, he'll give it to the earl."

Reed paused, his gaze skimming briefly over the heart-shaped face, the enormous doelike brown eyes framed by the mane of reddish-brown locks in need of a trim. The travel dress she wore was out of fashion and stained by the rigours of the trip from America.

He had learned ascending Charles's stairs ten minutes before that blond, curly-haired Rory was the daughter of Lady Pamela Spalding. He had assumed that the woman in front of him was Rory's governess.

"You must be famished," he said now, kindly. "Hardy will be glad to show you to the kitchen for a bite to eat." He smiled at her in the way that never failed to win favour among the servants in his own household and sauntered out the door, his mind filled with the Arabian he was charged with buying for his cousin.

"If you please, Miss..." Hardy rose to the occasion.

"Spalding," Vivian supplied, two spots of colour burning in her cheeks. She might not know the nuances of life in England, but she had no doubt that only servants ate in the kitchen.

Hardy's impenetrable mask slipped a fraction.

"Are you any relation to Lady Pamela Spalding, miss?"

"I am her stepdaughter. That gentleman who just left here, what is his name?"

"Do you mean Mr. Reed, miss? Mr. Lucian Reed."

A mere mister, not even a viscount or marquis or earl, and he had treated her like a servant! What would a real marquis or earl do to her?

As she stood, mulling over her fate, the door to the drawingroom opened and Rory sprang out.

"Oh, Viv, here you are. Come in, do. Grandfather wants to see you. And he's not an ogre even if he is an earl. And wait till you see Aunt Edwina. I shall need that letter from Mama, lest someone mistake us for a pair of downstairs maids. Why are you standing there? Come on!" she adjured, ushering her sister into the drawingroom to meet the earl and Lady Edwina, who, Viv hoped, would not immediately set her to work polishing the silver.

If Vivian had cause for legitimate complaint from the cavalier treatment of a mere Mister Reed, she had no complaint in the least at how the earl and Lady Edwina greeted her. Both were relieved to find a sensible female who could tell them what Aurora was doing in London, since the letter from Lady Pamela consisted of only one line: *Papa, I am sending you Aurora.*

As though, Vivian thought, Rory were nothing more than a barrel of sugar from a plantation.

She answered the earl's questions in her forthright manner, stating that if it were convenient with him they would spend part of the month with him in London and then perhaps move on to spend time with friends on the Continent. Lady Edwina she indulged with tales of the *mal de mer* both she and Rory had fallen prey to on the ship, a telling so authentic that Atwater was rendered a trifle green. The hoped-for effect was achieved causing Lady Edwina to send them abovestairs to rest while a tray with light broth and biscuits could be prepared for them.

"Oh Vivian, isn't this house grander than Mama's stories?" Rory exclaimed, as she bounced on the huge fourposter bed.

"Much grander," Vivian agreed. Indeed, one would have to be blind not to have seen the marble columns in the drawingroom, the exquisite Chinese vases in the hallway. Even their bedchamber held a charming painted ceiling the likes of which Philadelphia had never seen.

Perhaps that was the reason Lady Pamela had dispatched Rory and her to London, to show them to be American bumpkins. Well, it wouldn't happen. Not while Vivian was alive to protect Rory. Fortunately Vivian herself had been schooled in America by a very proper English governess who had taught her just what was done in England by a lady and what was not. Moreover there was Lady Pamela herself, whose speech was riddled with English expressions. She was forever succumbing to the vapours or flying into the boughs, and Vivian and Rory had both readily adopted her expressions into their own speech.

"I always thought Mama was prone to exaggerate," Rory said now, thumping a pillow with her fists. "But it is magnificent. What shall we do first?"

"First, we shall unpack," Vivian said, taking her question literally. "Then we shall eat, if anyone comes with that tray Lady Edwina promised, for I am famished."

"So am I. I do hope she brings more than just broth and biscuits."

Chattering amicably, the two sisters set to work, unpacking their portmanteaux.

They shook out and hung up the clothes they had brought from home, new purchases every one. Vivian, however, was obliged to admit that the dresses which had seemed just the thing in Philadelphia now looked dowdy hanging in the great wardrobe in their bedchamber.

The tray arrived just as they finished their unpacking. In the mood for a comfortable cose, Lady Edwina brought it up herself, and over a cup of Bohea tea she asked them about Philadelphia.

"When you go back to America you must take with you a tonic that I have. It is said to cure *mal de mer.*"

"Have you never felt the inclination to go to America yourself, ma'am?"

Lady Edwina recoiled in horror. "Why should I?"

"Well, you could visit Mama, for example," Rory said.

Lady Edwina, who correctly recalled her niece as a very spoiled brat, prone to dismissing all her advice and to laughing at her behind her back, was not tempted by a reunion.

"It is not hard to see why you prefer England, ma'am," Vivian interjected. "We've had only a glimpse of London. It is much grander than in the stories Lady Pamela used to tell."

"Oh yes. And you must see everything. Now that the two of you are here, we can go out to see the sights: the Tower of London, Madame Tussaud's Waxworks, and even the Zoo." She glanced at Rory. "How old are you, Aurora?"

"Eighteen."

"Are you out yet?"

"Out where?"

"Out of the schoolroom."

"I've had a governess and a tutor," Rory said proudly. "And Viv has taught me."

"Then you have made your come-out? With the two of you in London we could perhaps go out in the evening, to some of the soirées and balls. With just Charles and myself, it is cosier to stay in, but with two young ones like yourselves, it would be fun to see you in your finery."

Rory put down her soup spoon and clapped her hands. "Viv, did you hear! Isn't it exciting?"

"Yes, indeed," Vivian murmured.

"And the very first thing we shall do tomorrow is to take you to Fanchon. She is the best dressmaker in London. You cannot appear as you are in public."

"But who will pay for the clothes?" Vivian asked. "Aurora is the earl's granddaughter and might presume upon his generosity, but I have no such tie and cannot allow him to stand the cost."

"Good heavens, child, Charles is as rich as Golden Ball. It would do him a world of good to part with some blunt on the pair of you."

"But Lady Edwina—"

"You have no recourse but to say yes," Rory crowed with delight. "For if you say no, I shall not go to the dressmaker either, and Grandfather will be put to the blush at my appearance."

Knowing Rory, Vivian felt that she was fully capable of appearing in rags to get her way and gave her reluctant agreement, but she still did not like being beholden to anyone. It went against her American heritage.

CHAPTER TWO

AN ESTATE SALE WAS NEVER a happy occasion, Lucian Reed thought as he observed the possessions carted out of the attic and great rooms. Tapestries, paintings, tables and chairs were stacked up on the green lawn, while the bankrupt family waited nearby.

Stepping down from his barouche, Reed almost wished that he had bypassed the sale. But he had promised Charles to see if the Arabian was available. He found his way past the tear-stained eyes of the wife and felt the tug of his own unhappy memories.

He had been but a lad of ten when his own father had lost their estate, gambled away in a night of drunken excess. Reed had been packed off to live with an uncle, who had taken a liking to the young boy and educated him and taught him about the intricacies of the Exchange. Upon the death of his uncle, Reed had inherited a sizable fortune. But so vivid was the memory of the loss of the family home that he had meticulously avoided the temptation of cards and any type of wagering.

This left only the pursuits of fashion, females and sport to a gentleman like himself. His driving skill was enough to win him membership in the Four Horse Club, and he had at times received the personal attention of Jackson himself in the boxing saloon, but he could never be considered wholly addicted to sport. And since he did not dabble overmuch in the petticoat line, it was in matters of fashion that he most distinguished himself. Indeed, since Brummell's fall from favour, Reed was considered the most elegant man in London.

Consultation with one of the stable lads revealed that the Arabian had been sold. Reed took a quick turn about the stables but found nothing else that would interest a horse-mad earl like Charles.

He made his way to a nearby table and picked up a small wooden toy soldier.

"Here now, you can't take that," a voice protested.

Reed looked up into the hostile face of a ten-year-old boy.

"Now, hush," the woman silenced her son.

"Is it your soldier?" he asked the boy, who glared at him in mute fury.

The boy nodded.

"How much do you want for it?"

The boy looked at him defiantly. "Ten pounds."

"Willie! Pray not pay him any mind, sir," the woman said hastily, fearing that her son had spoiled the sale.

"Ten pounds was the stated price," Reed said, tossing a bag of coins at the woman. "The soldier is mine, then?"

"Aye, sir. It is."

"Then I choose to give it to William here," he said, handing the wooden toy back to the boy.

"Sir—"

"Reed, just the fellow who can help me!"

Reed turned to find one of his boon companions, Viscount Trawley, waving at him.

"Hold tight to that soldier," Reed told the young boy and went over to see what his friend wanted. The sturdy, sandy-haired viscount was just an inch shorter than Reed, with a neckcloth arranged now carelessly about his throat. The two men shared a predilection for sport, and Reed considered him a firm friend despite the viscount's unfortunate reputation as a rake.

Reed was not acquainted with the full particulars of his friend's rakish past, but he did not judge him too harshly.

Trawley might play fast and loose with their hearts, but females pursued him as much as he they.

"Egad, what are you doing up and about, George?" he asked now. "Can't be noon yet."

"Half past that, by my timepiece," his friend replied with a laugh. "Just see what I've found. Castor and Pollux."

"Castor and who?"

"Pollux, you gudgeon. The twins," Trawley explained as Reed examined the marble sculpture through his quizzing glass.

"But what are you going to do with it, them, the twins?"

"When I refurbish my country estate I am going to erect a sculpture garden. What do you think?"

"I think of the pieces here, that Mercury is better suited to a garden," Reed replied.

The viscount took a step back, comparing the fleet-footed Mercury to the twins.

"You are right. I wish I had your eye, Reed."

Reed gave the marble statue a push. It didn't budge.

"How do you plan to move it?" he enquired.

"Did you come on horseback?" his friend asked.

"No, by carriage."

"That's it, then. I'm on horseback. If you'll transport the sculpture home to London, I'll be grateful, Reed. Next week I shall take it to the country."

"What will Lady Fitzwilliam think of your new purchase?" Reed asked, after agreeing to transport the sculpture.

The viscount frowned. "Who the devil is Lady Fitzwilliam?"

"That consumptive female with the bays you were dangling after."

"Ah yes, the bays!" the viscount smiled as his memory was jogged. "Beautiful pair. Cost me a veritable fortune. Their owner is currently taking the waters in Cheltenham."

"The perfect restorative for a broken heart?" Reed hazarded a guess.

"Unfair!" his friend protested. "She set her cap at me. Besides, there is a happy ending. She is set to marry her cousin on the Continent."

"And that makes it all right?" Reed asked ironically.

Trawley smiled blithely at him. "Of course. For females marriage is the perfect restorative. Now, come and help me load this infernal statue!"

ALTHOUGH LADY EDWINA had attempted to obtain an appointment the next day for Vivian and Aurora with Madame Fanchon, the modiste had not been able to fit them into her busy schedule. Finally on Tuesday Vivian was ushered into the back room where Fanchon herself wielded the measuring tape and commanded her where to look. A tiny, birdlike woman, Fanchon nonetheless was the avowed genius of London dressmakers.

"A hundred pounds!" Vivian exclaimed as she stepped away from Fanchon's tape. "Good heavens, Lady Edwina, in Boston for a hundred pounds I could buy three dresses."

"And they would look as though you came from Boston," Fanchon sniffed, her Gallic temperament by no means flattered by this American upstart.

"Oh Madame Fanchon, she doesn't mean it," Lady Edwina said hastily. "She is just an American..." As though, Vivian thought, her Americanism were a dreaded disease.

Having smoothed the modiste's ruffled feathers, Lady Edwina drew Vivian aside.

"Now, my dear, you mustn't get in Fanchon's black books or there will be no saving you."

"But the cost, ma'am."

"No doubt it is a colonial trait to be frugal," Lady Edwina said. "I've never had the head for it myself, but you mustn't turn into a purse squeeze. Habits of economy are commendable when necessary, but Charles is a generous soul. He gave me leave to open his budget for the two of you." She beamed at Rory who was now being measured by Fanchon.

It was all very well for Rory to accept the earl's generosity, but Vivian believed in paying her own way, as much as possible.

"I've told you before—" she began.

"Your arrival has taken the earl's mind off his gout, and for that all of us in the household are grateful. Now, no more arguments. While Fanchon is dealing with Aurora, let us find the material for a ball gown."

"Ball gown? Lady Edwina, no! I cannot accept such a gift," Vivian said. Such a gown would cost the earth, she was very sure. "And anyway, there will be little need for one."

"*Au contraire.* Charles is thinking of giving a ball in honour of the two of you. You will need to look your finest. Now... perhaps the gold, what do you think?"

"The gold would better suit Rory," Vivian said.

"Perhaps you are right... I shall try it on her," she said, taking the bolt of fabric away with her.

Vivian ran her fingers over the cloth. Such rich and fine fabrics certainly must please. Her stepmother had described the gowns and the finery that she was accustomed to back in London, but Vivian had always thought that mere exaggeration. Now she knew it was not. Already this morning they had been to milliners and glovers, and everything cost a fortune. But a ball gown?

As she stood there, her mind teeming with numbers and the amount in her small reticule, she became aware that a lady and a gentleman were coming down the aisle towards her. The lady was undoubtedly a beauty in the Immaculata style: blue eyes with golden hair in a becoming Sappho. She was dressed elegantly, in a sky-blue walking dress with a scalloped hem. The dark-haired gentleman was a perfect complement, Vivian thought, until he turned his face her way, and she recognized Mr. Lucian Reed.

Cheeks flaming as she recalled their last encounter, she busied herself with the cloth and hoped that he would not see her. There would be no necessity for him to address someone he thought of as a governess. Indeed, Vivian noted with a quick sidelong glance, it was plain from the way Reed's companion was talking to him that she was in the habit of claiming all his attention.

"Lucian, do you really think this shade is best for me?"

"Undoubtedly. Green is a colour that few females can wear to perfection. In it you stand out."

She simpered happily. "Then I know I must look divine, for your opinion in fashion is without equal."

Lady Edwina emerged from the back room with Aurora.

"Vivian, Fanchon concurs about the gold silk. She says she will have Rory's gown finished by the end of the week."

"I vow my back aches from having to stand straight," Rory complained.

"Good morning, Lady Edwina," Reed said, sauntering over to them with his companion. "You know Miss Long, I trust?"

"Yes, of course," Lady Edwina said with a smile. "How is your mother? When last I heard she had an inflammation of the lungs."

"She is much recovered," Miss Long said in a dismissive way.

"And do allow me to present Miss Aurora Spalding, and her governess, isn't it?" Reed went on. "But I didn't quite get your name the other day, ma'am," he said with a winning smile.

Lady Edwina stiffened, and Vivian herself froze, but Rory broke into a peal of laughter.

"Oh, that's ridiculous! Vivian isn't my governess, she's my sister!"

"Your sister!" Reed looked at her in dismay. "Good heavens, I do beg your pardon."

"Don't, Mr. Reed. I'd sooner be thought a governess than an English gentleman with bad manners," Vivian declared on her way out the door.

"YOU MUST OWN, VIV, that it is amusing, him mistaking you for my governess!" Rory said with a laugh on their way back to Hill Street. "Why you're only four years older than I!"

These words did little to assuage Vivian's hurt feelings. Were all gentlemen like Reed? she wondered, and turned the question to Lady Edwina, who had sunk back against the velvet squabs, scarcely knowing what to say.

"Like Reed? Oh heavens, child, no."

"See!" Rory crowed.

"Lucian is far better mannered, drinks only in moderation and never gambles. And you must have noticed how handsome he is."

"I noticed," Vivian said softly, wishing that she had not. Then it would have been easier to take his insult in stride.

"In fact," came the reluctant admission from Lady Edwina, "Reed is considered one of the pillars of our Society."

"A pillar of your Society," Vivian echoed. Her heart dropped. What was she in for if an ill-mannered gentleman like Reed was considered the best London could offer?

While Lady Edwina was attempting to prevent Vivian's low opinion of Mr. Reed from spoiling her London visit, Reed himself was standing in Fanchon's shop, feeling at point non plus. He had not meant to give offence. Indeed, he had thought he was bestowing a favour on the American female by recognizing her. Most gentlemen wouldn't have deigned to speak to her if they thought she were a governess.

"An Englishman with bad manners, did you hear?" Astrid Long's voice drew him from his reverie.

"I believe the entire shop heard," Reed said drily.

"Such insolence is not to be borne. A more ill-mannered female I've yet to meet. If she were a governess she would soon feel the back of my hand."

"Be fair, Astrid," Reed replied, dipping two fingers into his porcelain snuff-box. "I did slight her, however inadvertently."

Astrid's eyes narrowed into slits. Her companion's distracted mood did not set well in her dish. Reed should be acting the devoted suitor, particularly since Fanchon's shop was an inevitable morning stop in the rounds of London's most eligible Beauties.

It was not her intention to spend the morning with a companion whose mind was on another female, particularly an American.

She held up two bolts of cloth. "Is this one too green?" she enquired. "I should hate to use too much of a good thing."

Reed, usually quite willing to indulge in vigorous discussion of any aspect of fashion, found himself curiously eager to leave Fanchon's.

"It's fine," he announced. "Have it cut in the Grecian style, and you shall resemble Artemis herself."

His comment had the desired effect of sending her over to consult with Fanchon on the matter.

Reed fingered a bolt of silk. Silver was not a colour that Astrid would look well in. However, Miss Vivian Spalding would. Her russet tresses would be a marked contrast to the silvery colour. He let the cloth drop back onto the table, frowning ever so slightly at the intrusion of Miss Spalding into his thoughts.

He was not the sort of gentleman who delighted in giving offence under the guise of civility. His mistake had been an honest one, but why in heaven had he assumed she was a governess? No one had introduced her, but then again, he realized, no one had had the opportunity. He had seen her protective manner towards Aurora, and judging by that and her dress, which was not up to fashion, had leapt to the premature conclusion that she was a governess.

"Reed, are you wool-gathering?" Astrid flittered back.

"This would be the best place for it, don't you think, my dear?" he replied.

"A penny for them."

"My thoughts? You may have them freely. I was trying to think of a way to apologize to Miss Spalding for mistaking her for a governess."

Miss Long screwed her nose up in dismay. "Apologize? Good heavens, Reed. You are without equal for your civility. The female insulted you. An English gentleman with bad manners, indeed."

"Yes, well, I am an English gentleman and my manners were less than pleasing with her."

"Your mistake was excusable. She certainly dressed the part of a governess. I'm shocked that Lady Edwina would accompany her, so ill-garbed was she. A more dowdy rig I've never seen. Don't you agree, Reed?"

"It was rather out of mode," he admitted.

"My dear Lucian, were it further out of mode the Haymarket vendors would not even buy it," she said, laughing heartily at her sally which so amused her that she was obliged to repeat it at length to all who ventured to enquire what could be so comical, particularly to her bosom bow, Lady Frayne.

Lady Frayne, a petite brunette with an unfortunate inclination to freckle, had come out last Season along with Astrid and had scored the notable hit of leading Lord Frayne to the altar. Her husband was at this moment relating to Reed the details of the boxing match he had observed on the Heath the other day. Since Frayne was as sporting mad as they come, this enabled Astrid time to recount the encounter between the American and Reed to her friend.

"What an ill-mannered toad, to say such a thing to dear Lucian. He is always so civil. If he took her for a governess, heaven knows what anyone else would have taken her for. A maid?"

"Oh, her manners are the least of it."

"You jest."

"You did not see her dress, at least four years out of date. Reed and I quite agree it was the dowdiest thing we've seen any respectable female wear."

"Then I do hope Lady Edwina doesn't bring her to my musicale Thursday evening," Lady Frayne fretted. "I invited the earl and his family, and if he brings the granddaughter and she brings her sister..."

"If she does, I shudder to think what the result may be. Lucian is not about to set foot in the same room with her."

"Heavens, he is put out, then?" Lady Frayne directed a look at Reed, who stood some distance away, listening with an expression of polite enthusiasm to her husband's tale of sport.

"And with good reason," Astrid declared. "He is greatly offended by her deeds and words."

"Well, the invitations are sent," Lady Frayne pointed out. "I cannot uninvite them. And to cancel the party would be a nuisance. I pray that Lady Edwina has the presence of mind to keep her home, but if she comes, I shall be so cold as to make obvious on whose side my loyalties lie."

"What were you and Barbara prattling about?" Reed enquired when Astrid had drifted back to him.

"About her musicale on Thursday night," Astrid said, waving farewell to her friends. "Are you attending?"

"I don't know."

Miss Long made a moue. "You must. It is bound to be delightful."

"Not if she plays that infernal harp of hers!" he retorted as he handed her into his barouche.

After promising to ride in the Park with Astrid later that afternoon, Reed drove away from her residence in Cavendish Square. His courtship of Miss Long had begun a year ago when he had spied her in the Assembly Room. Instantly he had recognized her as a diamond of the first water, blond and statuesque of build with the manner of a queen.

His attentions to her had been duly noted, and he became her most favoured suitor. A few times he had thought of popping the inevitable question but had hesitated to cross that Rubicon.

Nevertheless Miss Long met all his requirements in a wife: she was a woman of good birth, beautiful, fashionable.

Reed stopped at White's to peruse the journals in comfort, but no sooner had he entered the reading room than he found himself the target of the Bond Street beaux.

"Tsk, tsk, Reed." Mr. Victor Hall stood in the doorway, clucking his tongue. "Is this the way an English gentleman with no manners conducts his morning? You ought to be out doing something of import." He turned to the gentleman at his elbow. "What is it that people do in America, Bartholomew?"

Bartholomew Crabb spilled snuff on his top-boots as he inhaled a pinch.

"I have heard it said on good authority that they work."

"Work!"

"Work," Crabb replied.

"Pon rep, that's the worst thing I've heard yet."

"If the two of you are finished, I should like to read my paper in peace," Reed said.

"But you must give us some instruction. I mean, if she thinks you ill-mannered, what she will say about me?"

"Of whom are you speaking?" Reed enquired icily.

"Atwater's granddaughter's sister. Do I have the relationship correct? I should hate to take her for a governess!" Mr. Hall said and guffawed wildly, leaving Reed with no alternative but to put down his paper and quit the room.

He nearly retreated back into the room when he saw the earl advancing down the hallway, his gout-ridden foot having been sufficiently restored that he could walk on it with the help of a cane.

"Ah, Reed, the very man I wish to see. Have a bit of rum business to discuss with you."

"Charles, you'd best sit, before you fall. How is it that you can walk? I thought you'd be laid up for a week."

"Vivian, that's my granddaughter's sister, you know—half sister really, Spalding's other daughter—had this recipe for a poultice. Had one of the maids cook it up and would you know, it works."

"First a governess, now a poultice-maker!" Hall nudged Crabb with his elbow.

The earl turned a baleful eye their way. "I am desirous of a private word with Reed.... Pair of bran-faced pups! What is the club coming to?" Lord Atwater continued when he was alone with Reed.

"Then your foot no longer pains you?"

"Don't be a cake, Reed. Of course it pains me. But not enough to keep me in that house of females. Bad enough with just Edwina. But now two more. And Americans!"

"Inclined towards revolutionary principles, are they?" Reed asked sympathetically.

"Aye. Lucky you don't have a title to worry about. Now—" he looked straight at Reed "—enough about that. I've been waiting for you to come forward. What's your excuse, and it had better be good."

It came as no surprise to Reed that Charles had heard about the words he had exchanged with Miss Spalding.

"In perfect truth, Charles, I know I acted hastily. But how could I know that she was Miss Aurora's sister? It was a mistake, and I meant no offence by it."

A look of perfect bafflement suffused the earl's face.

"What's all this nonsense about Vivian? I want to know about my horse!" the earl expostulated. "You did go to Fernrod's estate sale?"

"Ah, yes," Reed said, hastily recalling the commission his cousin had given him. "So I did. That Arabian was sold. But I was reluctant to tell you so, since I knew how much you wanted it. Trawley told me about another stable with Arabians for sale, so I took the liberty of sending my man there to ask on your behalf. That's why I didn't see fit to tell you."

"Well, I hope to get an Arabian," the earl said, picking up a journal. "Now, what were you saying about begging Vivian's pardon and mine?"

"I'm afraid I insulted Miss Spalding by mistaking her for Miss Aurora's governess. No one had introduced us at your residence the other day. Aurora I knew was your granddaughter, and so I just assumed..."

The earl cocked a craggy eyebrow. "Governess, eh? Told Edwina she couldn't be taking them out in London in those Philadelphia clothes, but they would insist upon seeing the sights. Devilish awkward for you, I take it."

"It quite bowled me over, sir."

"I shall handle the matter for you. I'll tell Vivian that you are most dreadfully sorry about it. You are, aren't you? Sorry, I mean."

"Oh, yes."

"Well then, that's all right. She's a sensible female and I daresay she's forgot all about it."

CHAPTER THREE

VIVIAN SPALDING WAS a sensible female, a fact known widely in her native Philadelphia. However Lord Atwater had been mistaken in his assumption about the workings of that particular female's mind. When he apologized on Reed's behalf, he expected his American guest to accept the apology with good grace and have done with it. She acknowledged his words with a brief nod, but her smile and her flashing dark eyes made it clear that she was not entirely pleased.

"Well, of course, she's not pleased!" Lady Edwina declared later when the two of them were alone in the sitting-room. "The way you blundered in just now and gave her Reed's very rag-mannered apology! How idiotish that Lucian would mistake her for a governess. His mother's side of the family has always been deplorably short-sighted. That's the only possible explanation. Anyone blessed with two sound eyes and ears would know in a trice that Vivian is the equal of any lady in London."

"It's her dreadful style of dress," Lord Atwater said. "I hope to heaven Fanchon will attire her properly."

"She has promised the dresses by the end of the week."

"Good. Until then, perhaps you might confine them to the house," the earl said before retreating to his library. His bad foot began to twinge from all his racketing about.

"GRANDFATHER CAN'T mean it!" Rory exclaimed to Vivian later, when they were alone in their bedchamber. "How can he be so cruel? We are set to explore the Zoo tomorrow."

"Bother the Zoo, Rory. Can you imagine the gall of Reed tendering his apology to me through your grandfather? He knew quite well that I daren't refuse or say anything uncivil to the earl, who is our host."

"What would you have said if he had apologized himself?" Rory asked, flopping on the huge four-poster and propping her chin on her fists. Her blue eyes danced with glee.

Vivian paused, surveying herself in the gilt-edged mirror on the wall.

"I would have told him to jump in the Potomac. Or perhaps I should have said the Thames, since we are in London."

"Perhaps that's why he wouldn't come himself," Rory said sensibly. "He was afraid of you."

"That's nonsense," Vivian said. "He is not afraid of me. First, he thinks me a governess. Then I am of so little consequence, being an American female of no rank, not even a lady such as you may claim, that he does not apologize correctly. I am not stupid. I know how Londoners look down upon provincials and colonials. Mr. Reed undoubtedly shares those sentiments."

"But he seems quite charming to me."

Vivian threw her an affectionate glance. "You are related to the earl. I am not."

Rory jumped off the bed and gave her sister a vigorous hug.

"I am as American as you are."

"Yes, I know."

She did not divulge to Rory what she had been obliged to endure earlier that afternoon. Lady Edwina had been visited by two different callers, each of whom had coyly hinted about what Reed and his soon-to-be-betrothed Astrid Long had said on the matter of her wardrobe. *So outmoded the*

Haymarket vendors would not buy it! How she wished her purse were not so bare. She would have ordered a dozen dazzling dresses from Fanchon to take the wind out of Astrid's sails.

AT THAT VERY MOMENT Astrid Long was thinking not about sails but hats, particularly the new white riding hat she wore to match the white mare on which she was mounted. She turned her head enquiringly toward her companion on the black steed next to her.

"Ought I to wear it at this angle?" she asked Reed for what had to be the tenth time since they entered the Park.

"It looks lovely as it is," he said, as he had said nine times previously.

"I still think a little lower down on my brow..." Astrid angled the hat further, which made it prodigiously difficult for her to see. Reed was obliged to lay a hand on her reins to stop or start her horse.

In this curious manner they rode down the path, just as a carriage driven by Trawley approached from the opposite direction.

"A vehicle is coming," Reed said, slowing her horse.

"Is it anyone I know?" Astrid asked, peering up from under her hat.

"Lord Trawley."

Astrid sniffed. Trawley was not a favourite with her.

"Good afternoon, George," Reed hailed his friend.

"Good afternoon, Lucian, and Miss Long. It *is* Miss Long beneath that hat, I take it?" he quizzed.

Astrid lifted her head. "It is."

"How did Mercury fit into your sculpture garden?" Reed asked his friend.

"Very well. You know I have Poseidon and Athena. I daresay I could fit a whole pantheon of gods in the garden."

"No room for people."

"There will be room. Wait till you see my plans!" Trawley said, "I'm preparing the chapel."

"Chapel!" Reed expostulated. "Do you mean a church?"

"Naturally, a church," Trawley said, looking offended. "Every great house must have a chapel."

"Mr. Reed." Astrid's arctic voice interrupted the two laughing gentlemen. "I fear I must ask that we proceed up the pathway. My horse will get chilled in this wind."

"Why don't you sit in the carriage with me," Trawley suggested. "You shan't feel the wind then."

Astrid recoiled. It was the fashionable hour at the Park. She had wished to be seen at her best, and certainly not in the company of a rakehell like Trawley. A lady could not be too careful about the company she kept.

"Thank you, I'd as lief ride where I am," she said stiffly.

"Then I'll follow you home," the viscount said, making her an elaborate bow. He enjoyed twitting the conventions of Society's ladies, and no one was more hopelessly starched up than Astrid Long. She was a Beauty all right, though a bit of a Long Meg for his tastes, and he'd often wondered what Lucian saw in her.

Reed led their exodus out of the Park and towards Cavendish Square. With obvious reluctance Miss Long invited both gentlemen in to tea, an invitation which was swiftly declined.

"I don't think your Beauty likes me overmuch, Lucian," the viscount observed as the oak door closed behind her.

Reed clapped him on the shoulder. "In truth, Astrid likes few people."

"She likes you, though."

Reed considered the matter. He supposed she did. She made plain that she liked his ideas on fashion and what became her.

"Enough about Astrid. Tell me about this chapel of yours!"

THE NEXT MORNING the grounds of the Zoo echoed with the squeals of laughing children running from one exhibit to the next and with the voices of their beleaguered elders trying vainly to keep up with them.

Amidst the prams and bouncing balls, Vivian strolled with Lady Edwina and Rory. Though a cool wind blew, the sun shone brightly and her step was light. For once she felt utterly relaxed. Here, with the children and the animals, no one cared a jot that her Philadelphia garments were out of mode.

No word of rebuke came from the camel, thoughtfully chewing and casting a baleful eye at the spectators. She sauntered over to the ostrich cage, marvelling that those same feathers, dyed to a brilliant colour, might soon bedeck some lady's hat.

"Oh, Vivian, isn't this famous?" Rory exclaimed. "We have nothing like it in Philadelphia. I'm so glad the earl relented and we could come out today."

"It is splendid," she agreed. "Although I feel sorry for the animals. That poor ostrich. I vow whenever I see a lady with an ostrich feather, I shall think of him being plucked."

"They aren't plucked really," Lady Edwina intervened. "The feathers fall off."

They moved towards the exhibit of bears, laughing at the two shambling creatures, one black and one white. Next came the tigers and the leopards, but Vivian's favourite was the monkey cage. She laughed as the dear little creatures climbed all over the cage.

"These came from Africa," Rory said, reading the sign. "I should like to travel there someday."

Lady Edwina shuddered. "I shouldn't. Only think how arduous the trip would be, over the water."

"We crossed the Atlantic on our own," Rory pointed out. "In fact, Vivian and I are seasoned travellers."

"Not too well seasoned, I should hope," a voice said behind them, and the two sisters turned to discover Mr. Lucian Reed standing with another gentleman.

"Ah, Reed," Lady Edwina said with a flutter. She darted a quick look at Vivian, who seemed to be struck dumb by his appearance. "What are you doing here? The Zoo is the last place I would have thought to see you."

"It was Trawley's doing," Lucian drawled, bowing to the ladies and indicating the gentleman standing next to him. "He has this absurd idea of raising peacocks at Trawle, his country estate. I tried to tell him that despite their pretty appearance they give out the most dreadful cry in Christendom. And to prove it, I brought him along to find a peacock. But there is never a peacock about when one has need of one," he complained. "Oh, you haven't been properly introduced, have you, George? Miss Vivian Spalding and Miss Aurora Spalding. George Helprin, Lord Trawley."

The viscount bowed.

"Charmed."

"My lord," Vivian murmured. Trawley was about an inch shorter than Reed, but she liked the twinkle in his dark eyes.

"I hope that introduction was an improvement on my previous introduction the other day," Reed said, taking advantage of Edwina engaging Trawley in conversation to step closer to Vivian.

"Any introduction would be an improvement, sir," she replied, the colour high in her cheeks as she turned and walked towards the lion exhibit.

Now he had done the thing, Reed thought, cursing himself. It seemed that whenever he attempted to speak to Vivian he made a muddle of it. Why was that? She was a perfectly ordinary young lady.

Attempting to repair the damage, again he stepped quietly up to her, watching the lion stretch his paws lazily towards them.

"Didn't Charles relay my regrets about our unfortunate encounter?" he asked, cocking his head. The wind had blown a strand of hair across her cheek, and he resisted the urge to touch it.

"He made your apologies, if that is what you mean," Vivian said, turning to look at him and then immediately regretting that action. The blue-grey of his eyes reminded her of the Atlantic she had crossed so recently, and now they were piercing and quizzical. He was so very handsome, quite the top of the trees in a coat of fawn-coloured superfine and matching trousers. His Hessians gleamed in the sunlight, and she had no doubt that the neckcloth fashioned about his neck had taken the better part of an hour to perfect.

And she *would* have to be wearing another of her dowdy Philadelphia dresses. "I would think that English gentlemen would make their own apologies, but then I am an American and not used to your Town manners."

His smile faded, and his slender fingers toyed with the fob on his pocket watch. "I beg pardon. Charles assured me that you would not take umbrage if he performed my apologies. But I am most sincerely sorry for mistaking you for a governess the other day. Pray forgive me?"

After receiving this apology, Vivian could do little except assure Reed that he was forgiven for that mistake.

"For *that* mistake?" Reed asked, frowning slightly. "Have I made any other since then?"

She rubbed the iron railing with the tip of her gloved finger, not wishing to relive the mortification his comments had sparked within her.

His face, creased with concern, pressed closer, and she took a step back.

"Believe me, Miss Spalding, I am here to apologize for all my transgressions. Will you tell me what I've done? I don't like being in your black books."

His words were so sincerely expressed that Vivian believed him.

"You have been rather free with your speech to your friends, Miss Long and Lady Frayne, sir," she said finally.

"If you're talking about that introduction, I apologize again."

"I am also talking about your comments about my person," she said slowly. " 'Haymarket vendors,' indeed."

His brow knit further in puzzlement. "I don't understand."

Her gaze swept over his face. "Your opinion of my dress is all over London, sir," she said quietly. " 'So dowdy a rig, so out of mode that if it were any further out no Haymarket vendor would buy it!' "

Her words scored an uncomfortable hit and he squirmed, recalling Astrid's remarks and the laughter that had greeted them at Fanchon's. It was on the tip of his tongue to deny that he himself had uttered them. But a gentleman never discredited a lady to another.

"I am sorry that those words were ever uttered," he said sincerely. "You shall hear no further comments about your dress from my lips. You may don sackcloth and ashes and it would be all the same to me."

Trawley strolled over. "Reed, if you are through with the lions' cage we are going to find some refreshment. I think they have ices and lemonade but no champagne. Perhaps we'll see a peacock soon," he said, falling into step with Vivian. "Have you seen any about, Miss Spalding?"

"The only peacock I have observed today has been Mr. Reed," Vivian said with a smile.

The viscount clapped his friend on the back. "A splendid hit, Miss Spalding. And peacock, Lucian certainly is. The unfeathered variety. You must know that he is the most fashionable man in all London."

"Really?!" Vivian said, slightly taken aback.

"Since Brummell fled to the Continent, the role of supreme arbiter of fashion has fallen on Lucian's broad shoulders."

"I don't think Miss Spalding is interested in my broad shoulders, George."

"But I am!" Vivian said, then flushed slightly, hoping that her remark would not be misinterpreted.

"Lucian is too modest. Some in Society don't even bother to dress until they've consulted him."

"That's doing it too brown!" Reed expostulated. "Miss Spalding will think me a fashionable fribble."

"Oh, but I think it quite a feather in your cap to have such a position," Vivian responded, falling into the spirit of the thing. "In fact I believe that were you to adopt a feather anywhere on your person, it would soon be the rage."

"Do you think so?" the viscount asked, quite diverted by this idea. He stood aside and raised his quizzing glass. "Do you mean a feather cloak, like those the Sandwich Islanders wear?"

"Anything would do," Vivian said. "Any fashion he sports would bound to be adopted by all fashionable gentlemen."

"I wager you're right. What do you say, Lucian?"

"I never wager, you know that," Reed replied.

His answer prompted a look of surprise from Vivian. "Never, sir?"

"Oh, never," the viscount answered for his friend. "Reed never gambles and is the only man who goes to White's or Watier's for the company instead of the play at the green baize tables."

"Not even cards, sir?" Vivian asked, intrigued. Her father had taught her the rudiments of card-playing at a very early age.

"Particularly not cards," Reed replied, tightening his lips.

"Well then, Miss Spalding and I shall make the wager ourselves," Trawley said, dispatching this obstacle in his path. "You hold that if he sports some feathered garment, within a fortnight it will be the rage?"

Vivian nodded.

"I hold the same opinion, but for the purposes of the bet shall hold the opposite. Now what shall we wager? A hundred pounds?"

"That's rather dear," Vivian said, daunted by the sum quoted.

Trawley snapped his fingers. "I have a better suggestion. If you win I shall grant you any favour you like. Tickets to the Opera or Drury Lane, or what you will. And if I win, which I can't, really, for we both know that within a day the tulips will be aping Reed's lead, I shall ask a favour of you."

Reed frowned. Trawley was his friend, and he had never worried overmuch about the viscount's rakish reputation. But he couldn't help wondering what favour Trawley anticipated extracting from Miss Spalding.

"George, I think this fustian nonsense has gone far enough," he said.

Vivian ignored the interruption. "The wager is set, my lord," she said, holding out her hand to the viscount, who surprised her—and Reed—by kissing it.

Reed glared at his friend, conscious of a pang of envy. Was he intending to set up Miss Spalding as his flirt?

"I think you should reconsider," Reed said now.

"Don't worry, Reed, I shall fashion you the feathered garment myself."

"Good Jupiter!"

"Now shall we make the feathers peacock or ostrich?" Trawley asked, deep in thought.

"Peacock, of course," Vivian replied.

"If the two of you are finished with your preposterous suggestions..." Reed interrupted once again.

"What suggestions are these?" Rory demanded. She had dawdled behind with Lady Edwina to look at the lion cubs and only now overheard the conversation.

"A feathered garment for Lucian to wear," Trawley explained. "Miss Spalding declares it would be the rage within a week. We have a bet to that effect."

"Vivian has a wager with you, my lord?" Lady Edwina asked, feeling faint, and not from her walk with Rory.

"Yes. She'll win, of course, and then I shall be at her disposal."

"And if he wins I shall be at his disposal," Vivian said with a merry laugh, which Lady Edwina did not share.

Neither did Mr. Lucian Reed.

An hour later, after consuming a good number of cakes and tarts and several glasses of lemonade, the viscount took Rory and Lady Edwina off to make one last attempt at finding a peacock, and Reed made one more attempt to dissuade Vivian from the bet.

"Are you afraid to put your fashionable lead to the test, Mr. Reed?" she teased, her mood lightened by the refreshment and, she had to admit, his company.

"That is the least of my concerns," he said. "You are a very green girl. How old are you, anyway?"

"I am nearly twenty-two, and don't change the subject. You are just annoyed that we are wagering about you. For once you shall be the object of sport."

"I pray that I am the *only* object of sport which results from this wager," he said.

Trawley returned with what he called a delicious idea for the fashioning of the feathered garment.

"A headband, what do you think?"

Vivian laughed. "He will look like the Indians back in America."

"Perfect. That is an excellent suggestion. A headband, just like the Indians in America wear. And I have another notion."

"I pray you, spare me your nacky notions," Reed said wearily.

But his plea fell on deaf ears.

"Not just one type of feather but different varieties. A peacock feather, an ostrich feather, a chicken, a swan, a duck. What do you think, Miss Spalding?"

"I think it will be just the thing," Vivian said, smiling broadly as she thought of the handsome Mr. Reed wearing such a headpiece.

As the Atwater carriage sped back to Hill Street, Lady Edwina's mind teemed with stratagems to explain the wager to the earl. It was goose to guineas he would hear about it. Her conscience teased her. She should have done something, but she couldn't really explain to Vivian in Lord Trawley's presence about his dreadful reputation with females. There had been that episode with the Bradley chit he was supposed to have ruined years before. Lady Edwina gave him the benefit of the doubt in that case, for Miss Bradley had been a headstrong and hoydenish female.

There had been other incidents rumoured about during the years. But Trawley was so charming that Lady Edwina usually forgot until much later that she was conversing with a rake.

The carriage rolled along the cobble-stoned street, and Lady Edwina's gaze slid towards the two sisters on the seat opposite. Vivian would have not a shred of reputation left if she lost the bet with Trawley. "Grant him any favour he wished," indeed. Lady Edwina shuddered, dug into her reticule for her hartshorn and held it to her nose.

"Are you feeling faint, ma'am?" Vivian turned with some concern to Rory's aunt.

"Oh no, child. It's just that this wager with Trawley has me in a pelter."

Vivian's eyes widened in surprise. "But there is nothing to fear, ma'am. I won't lose."

"How can you be so certain?" Lady Edwina asked.

"You said it yourself, ma'am. Reed is a pillar of your Society. And Trawley says he is the leader of fashion. Where he leads, few men would hesitate to follow, even—" her brown eyes danced with amusement "—in a feathered headband."

Lady Edwina was not so convinced. Fretfully, she pulled at the strings of her reticule, hoping that no one would find out about the wager. But that was wishing after stars. Once Reed walked down Bond Street in one of those Indian headbands, questions would arise. She gazed at her two young companions. Not for the first time, she felt helpless in the face of her American guests.

She had wished to obtain vouchers for them but had fought shy of calling on the Patronesses until the young ladies were suitably dressed by Fanchon and could be seen to advantage. But would any of the Patronesses bestow the prized vouchers once they learned about the wager with Trawley?

The excursion to the Zoo had seemed such an innocuous outing. Yet now she found herself fretting as their carriage slowed in traffic.

"You should have seen Trawley chasing the peacock, Viv," Rory said. "I was in whoops."

"And we shall be in whoops once more when we see Mr. Reed wearing the headband which Trawley has promised to make for him," her sister answered, chuckling again at that vision in her mind.

Finally their carriage reached the flagway on Hill Street. Lady Edwina descended, wanting nothing more than to take to her bed, but she was not to receive that yearned-for respite. Coming down the stairs from the earl's residence was none other than the august Lady Jersey.

Lady Jersey, a Patroness at Almack's, had an avowed weakness for turbans. She wore one now, a purple confection held in position by an amethyst pin and punctuated by one very long ostrich plume. Upon catching sight of it, both Spalding sisters howled with laughter.

CHAPTER FOUR

"Peacock, ostrich, swan, chicken, and duck. All awaiting Davidson to stitch them into a headband for you, Lucian." Lord Trawley grinned as he glanced up from the five feathers on his mahogany table.

Seated in a curricle chair, Reed leisurely inhaled a pinch of snuff.

"Davidson will think you foxed."

"None the less he shall do it if I pay him. He's Prinny's tailor and welcomes clients who can pay their bills on time."

The viscount picked up a chicken feather and blew on it.

Reed snapped shut his Sèvres snuff-box. He loved a good jest as well as the next man, but enough was enough.

"I would welcome it if you would put aside this wager, George," he said, rising to pace on the viscount's prized Wilton.

"This whole thing has got out of hand," Reed continued. "Miss Spalding is an exuberant American female who might not know better, but you certainly should."

Trawley gave his head a sad shake. "Lucian, you have been in the company of that dreary Astrid for too long. She has never had a sense of the ridiculous, and now you don't, either."

Reed paused in midstride. "Astrid is not dreary, and she has nothing to do with this. The Spalding sisters do."

"Yes, delightful creatures, didn't you think? Not an ounce of conceit between them, unlike most females. Of course they could both do with new dresses."

"Pray do not mention their dresses to me," Reed said, holding up both hands in mock surrender.

The viscount put down the chicken feather.

"What is amiss, Lucian? I know you frown on wagering—"

"That's not the point."

"You were not this alarmed over the wager I placed with Fogarty, which forced me to race to York and back with one hand tied behind my back."

"This is different."

"How so?" the viscount asked quietly.

Reed stared at his friend, loath to give offence, but duty-bound to clear the air.

"Your reputation with the ladies is well known, George."

Trawley grimaced. "A rather sanctimonious attitude, my friend."

"What do you think the quizzes will say when they learn of the terms of your wager? You shall grant Miss Spalding a favour of her asking if you lose, and she shall do the same."

"Calm yourself, Reed. I don't plan to ask her for her virtue."

Reed snorted. "I know that! But people will prattle all the same."

"People will say and think what they will, haven't you learned that yet?" the viscount asked, his dark eyes flashing with temper. "I have yet to find any way to stop a rumour that the gossip-mongers wanted repeating. A man might turn blue in the face if he tried it. I know whereof I speak," he said, looking grim. "That Bradley chit thought she had caught me in her trap, and when I refused to play the game, I was denounced as a blackguard." He shrugged and then shook his head as though to clear the memory.

"And speaking of reputation—mine may be in shreds, but Miss Spalding's will be intact if yours is on the mark."

"Mine?"

"As a supreme arbiter of fashion," Trawley quizzed, his good humour now restored. "Come along, let's see what Davidson can make of this headband of yours!"

LAUGHING UNWITTINGLY AT Lady Jersey's feathered turban had been a grave error, Vivian discerned immediately. Her face crimson, Lady Jersey stalked away from the earl's residence with Lady Edwina scurrying after her. The ostrich feather on the purple turban swayed back and forth in the wind.

"Oh, Rory, I fear we have behaved like a pair of ramshackle creatures," Vivian said, leading her sister into the blue drawingroom.

This fear increased when Lady Edwina returned without Lady Jersey. Vivian felt an immediate pang of remorse. Dear Lady Edwina had taken them under her wing, had shown them about London, not seeming to care about their dowdy rigs. And now they had offended her friend.

"Oh, my dears, how I wish you had not done that!" she said now in a voice of mild complaint.

"I do beg your pardon, Lady Edwina. We are a pair of hoydens, aren't we? And our manners are abominable. Pray, tell me the name of your friend and I shall pen her as pretty an apology as I am capable of."

"She's not a friend, she's a Patroness," Lady Edwina said in the voice of one inured to misfortune. "The Patronesses are all so high in the instep that there is no bearing them. But Sally Jersey was always a bit kinder than the others. I so hoped to convince her to procure vouchers for the two of you. Now it's hopeless."

"Vouchers for what?" Rory asked, picking absentmindedly at the tea-tray.

"Vouchers for Almack's," Lady Edwina said. "Oh, heavens. You probably don't even know what Almack's is."

"We are dreadfully ignorant," Vivian acknowledged, "but you must realize we have only been in London a sennight."

"Has it been a sennight?" Lady Edwina mused, accepting the biscuit that Rory offered her on a silver plate. "It seems much longer."

"Because of the trials you have been put to," Vivian said, unable to fully hide a mischievous smile. "But do tell us more about Alma's, ma'am."

"Not Alma's. *Almack's*. And it's simply the most exclusive club in London for eligible young ladies to meet the most eligible gentlemen."

"Are the rooms very grand?" Vivian quizzed.

"Well, no," Lady Edwina admitted. "Or at least no grander than other Assembly rooms."

"I suppose then that the refreshments are without equal anywhere?"

Here Lady Edwina was obliged to admit that the refreshments consisted usually of stale cakes and sour lemonade.

Rory made a face. "Then why should anyone go there?"

"Rory's right," Vivian said. "I have lived twenty-one years without setting foot in Almack's, and I daresay I shall survive another twenty-one years without it."

"Yes, but then you were in America. Here in London it is different. And if you are to have a future here in London you must be accepted at Almack's."

Later that afternoon, as Vivian sat in her bedchamber perusing a copy of *La Belle Assemblée,* Lady Edwina's words echoed in her mind. A future in London? She had willingly accompanied Rory to England believing that they would return to Philadelphia one day. But what if the earl, who had rapidly become attached to Rory, wished his granddaughter to remain here. What would Viv do then? Return to America alone?

She glanced down at the sketch of a lady in Grecian-style dress. The blond woman reminded her of Reed's friend,

Astrid Long. She wondered how serious was their attachment. Had the banns been posted? Then she shook her head. Reed's nuptials were none of her business, but Rory was.

Though she was fond of her country, she was fonder of Rory.

Pushing the magazine away abruptly, she crossed the sittingroom to the small escritoire. She sharpened a quill and then dipped it into the ink.

"What are you doing?" Rory asked when she came in to find Vivian blotting and sealing the letter.

"I am writing a letter of apology to Lady Jersey," Vivian said. "Our conduct was inexcusable."

"Oh, fiddlesticks. Aunt Edwina just worries too much."

"And with good reason. We have behaved like countrified dowds." Vivian marched out into the hall, summoned a footman, and dispatched him to deliver the letter to Lady Jersey's residence.

"Such a fuss over a purple turban," Rory complained when Vivian returned to the sittingroom.

"Wouldn't you like to go to Almack's?"

"Do you mean the place with the sour lemonade?" Rory wrinkled up her nose. "No. Would you?"

Vivian paused in thought.

"It will probably be very different from anything we've seen in Philadelphia."

"Everything in London is different from Philadelphia," Rory retorted. She picked up her sister's discarded magazine and thumbed through it. "It's so grand. There is so much to see and do. Plus there's Grandfather and Aunt Edwina."

"You like them, then?"

"Why, yes. Grandfather especially, when the gout isn't upon him. He has been telling me all about our family history. We shall see his country seat next month."

"Next month?"

"Yes," Rory answered. "That will be June. No one remains in London during the summer. It is mauvais ton."

Vivian smiled at Rory's easy adoption of London expressions.

"Your grandfather said that, did he?"

"No, actually it was Lord Trawley. He is so amusing, and he is building a country home not far from Atwater, Grandfather's estate. So if we do go there we shall undoubtedly see a good deal of the viscount."

Vivian's original plans for the summer in no way coincided with the ones Rory had just related. She intended to stay a month in London, and assumed that afterwards they would go on to the Continent. "Has your grandfather invited you to his country home?"

Rory nodded. "This will probably be the most pleasant summer we shall have. Mama won't be about to pinch and scold us. Grandfather is such a pet, when his gout is not bothering him, and Aunt Edwina, well, I've just never known anyone kinder, have you?"

"No," Vivian admitted. Rory's English family was all she could hope for.

LOVING AND GRACIOUS though she might be, Lady Edwina was no shatterbrain. By succumbing to a mild touch of the grippe she prevented her guests from attending Lady Frayne's musicale, thus sparing them Lady Jersey's wrath.

The absence of the Americans was a disappointment not only for Lady Jersey, who had wished to stigmatize the pair as country bumpkins to her fellow Patronesses, but also to Miss Long, who wanted to turn them a cold shoulder in public.

"Americans are so gauche," Astrid explained to Mr. Clive, the dandy who was inspecting the lace-trimmed sleeves of her gown of sea-water green satin through his quizzing glass. "I have heard tell that they are gadding about London, oblivious to the very odd appearance they make in their old clothes."

"I hear they went to the Zoo," Mr. Clive tittered. "Perhaps they wore their best for the animals."

"Do you know who they went there with?" Miss Barret, a pretty brunette who had been shamelessly eavesdropping, now put in. "Trawley."

"What?"

Miss Barret nodded eagerly. "Oh, yes. I had it straight from my sister's nanny, who is in the habit of taking her charges to the Zoo. It was Trawley. There was another gentleman, too, with him, but Nanny unfortunately is so short-sighted that she could not recognize him from the distance. But Trawley passed right before her chasing a peacock."

"The Spaldings are not only ignorant but troublesome," Astrid declared. "Everyone knows Trawley is a loose screw."

"Lucian Reed seems to like him," Mr. Clive observed.

"Lucian is too charitable by half," Astrid said with a sniff. "I shall cure him of that when we are married. And once we are married Trawley shall not darken our door."

"Has Reed made you an offer, then?" Miss Barret asked.

Miss Long hesitated for just a fraction of a second. "Not yet. But soon, my dear, very soon."

"If he's going to pop the question, where is he?" Mr. Clive asked with another titter. "He is not attending you this evening?"

"No." Miss Long pursed her lips. Reed had not given in to her entreaties to accompany her to the musicale. She was somewhat put out by his declaration that listening to harp music inevitably gave him a headache and he would not suffer such a penance for all the gold in Christendom.

Astrid was not overly fond of music either, but the musicale was an opportunity for her to receive compliments and hence she would not miss it.

The absent Mr. Reed found himself the next morning with a headache every bit as punishing as those inflicted by Lady Frayne's harp.

Davidson had stitched the infernal headband, and Trawley had hauled him up from his bed to try it on. The viscount found his friend surprisingly amenable to taking part in the hoax.

"Had a change of heart, did you?" he asked. "Why's that?"

"To save Miss Spalding from your clutches," he joked, though it wasn't entirely a joke. The American did not seem to know what a dangerous game she was playing, and for some reason he felt duty-bound to keep an eye on her. As for his influence on fashion, he knew quite well that idiotish tulips would adopt the feathered look if he sported it.

"It is too small," he pointed out, as the band refused to slip over his crown and around his forehead.

"That's easily remedied," Trawley said cheerfully, setting to work on the headband as Reed dressed. "Perhaps it's your hair. We can cut some of it off."

"Oh, we can, can we?" Reed said dangerously. "I advise you not to test my patience, George. Touch one lock of my hair and I shall dump you in the Thames." His fingers never strayed from the intricate knot he was tying in his neckcloth.

"Your hair is safe for now," the viscount said, settling back with the scissors and the headband. He ripped out the stitches Davidson had sewn. "Now try it on...."

Trawley had indeed solved the problem of the headband being too small. It was now too big, slipping down the bridge of Reed's nose.

"It's either too big or too small," Trawley said. "Devilish coil. I have it!" he exclaimed and began to rummage in his friend's wardrobe.

Reed watched in amusement as his friend finally emerged with one of Mr. Locke's famous beaver hats.

"What are you doing?" Reed asked, his amusement turning to alarm.

"Watch this," the viscount said, his fingers already slipping the headband over the crown of the hat. "What do you see?"

"I see the most preposterous hat in the kingdom!" Reed began to laugh.

"Try it on."

A minute later Reed gazed into the looking-glass. From the neck down he appeared every inch the London gentleman with the faultlessly knotted Trône d'amour, champagne-buffed Hessians and one of Weston's finer waistcoats.

But above the neck was another story.

The hat had been one of Mr. Locke's simplest designs, for Reed favoured little ornamentation in hats. But now feathers jutted out every which way. The ostrich plume was so long he would have to bend double to get into a closed carriage.

"Oh, first-rate, Lucian," Trawley crowed. "Now where shall you be seen in it? Shall I take you over to Miss Spalding immediately?"

"Good God, no!" Reed said. He tossed the hat onto the bed and quitted the dressingroom. The viscount followed him down the Adam staircase carrying the hat. In the breakfast parlour the two men partook of a hearty morning meal of ham and sausage and three different kinds of bread.

"It will be such sport to see if Miss Spalding is right," Trawley said. "Can you imagine all London wearing such things?"

"That would be a sight," Reed agreed on the broad grin.

Finley, the butler, appeared just then to announce Miss Long, who swept into the room as though she were already its chatelaine.

Her smile froze when she saw Trawley.

"Good day, Miss Long," the viscount said.

She inclined her head a fraction. "My lord." She turned to Reed. "Give me leave to tell you your absence last night was noted by many."

"Acquit Reed," Trawley replied before his friend could speak. "It was my fault. We were in the midst of a quandary last evening, one which persists even to this morning, on a point of fashion."

"Fashion?" Astrid couldn't help betraying a flicker of interest at Trawley's words.

"Yes, perhaps you could assist us."

"George," Reed warned in an undertone, but the viscount ignored him.

"I am always glad to lend my expertise to those wishing advice," Astrid said with a simper.

The viscount had been holding Reed's hat behind his back and now presented it to Lady Astrid, who shrank back against her chair.

"What is that?" she enquired.

"A feathered hat for gentlemen."

"Indeed?" she asked sceptically, eying it with some suspicion. "Yours, I presume?"

"No, it's Reed's."

"Really?" She turned towards Reed, who was pouring himself some coffee. "Is that true, Lucian?"

"Yes, the hat is mine."

"Davidson stitched the feathered band yesterday for us," the viscount said conversationally. "And this morning we hit on the idea of putting it over one of Reed's beaver felts. What do you think of it?"

Few would dispute Reed's rank in matters of fashion, particularly Astrid. His attraction for her was based mostly on his position as an exquisite. Together, she was convinced, they constituted the most fashionable couple in London. And were they to marry and produce children, she was sure they would be the most fashionable children in all of England.

Hence, she did not quarrel in the least with the feathered hat if Reed was thinking of adopting it.

"Why don't you put it on, Reed? Miss Long can get a more accurate picture of how you will look."

Certain that Astrid would be convulsed with laughter within seconds, Reed donned Mr. Locke's now altered masterpiece.

"Stunning, my dear Reed," the viscount pronounced. "What think you, Miss Long?"

"Quite striking," she agreed. "The contrast in colours is without equal."

"You have heard the lady, Reed," Trawley exclaimed, his eyes dancing. "I trust you will let London see you in it soon. But not just for a stroll down Bond Street. I have it: you shall appear in the Park at the fashionable hour. That would be the perfect time to be seen in it, don't you think, Miss Long?"

Reed's gaze rested on the blond Beauty. Could Astrid seriously think such a headpiece was fashionable?

"I think it is splendid," Astrid agreed. "In fact I shall be there myself."

"WHY THE DEVIL did you do that?" Reed complained after she had departed.

"Why not? She loved your hat, so..." Trawley struggled to contain himself, but finally exploded in gales of laughter. "Reed, you are going to be leg-shackled to a fashionable bird-wit."

Reed frowned. "Astrid is not blue, but she is no bird-wit."

The viscount looked up quickly, a sober expression in his eyes. "Meant no offence."

"Good." Astrid might be a lady of fashion, but there was surely more to her than just clothes and jewellery, just as there was more to Reed than the tying of a neckcloth. For Astrid's sake and his own, he would find a way of proving that, once and for all.

CHAPTER FIVE

LAUGHING WOULD LAND HER in the suds, Vivian told herself as she clapped a gloved hand over her mouth. Her sides ached with the suppressed laughter, and she knew that Rory was similarly afflicted as they both peered through the window of the earl's closed carriage. Just as Trawley had predicted, there was Reed riding on his black steed, wearing the hat the viscount had concocted.

When Reed tipped the feathered hat at a passing lady, and the huge ostrich feather tickled the woman under her chin, Vivian was unable to control herself any longer. She began to laugh. Rory, relieved, soon joined her and the two sisters sat with tears streaming from their eyes.

"I vow, no more! It positively hurts," Rory said when she could finally speak.

A rap on the door to the carriage interrupted Vivian's reply. She glanced out the window, taken by surprise to see none other than Reed himself, feathered hat securely resting upon his dark hair.

"Well, Miss Spalding, are you satisfied?" he quizzed.

"Good afternoon, sir," she said, surprised by his cordial mood. She'd expected him to be more peevish.

"You look quite the top of the trees, Mr. Reed," Rory volunteered.

"Yes, a notable swell," Vivian said, choking on a laugh.

Reed smiled. At least they knew he looked ridiculous in the hat. Other females hadn't. The whole affair reminded him of that fairy-tale about the emperor's new clothes.

"Did anyone ask why you were wearing the feathered hat?" Vivian asked.

"Indeed they did," he retorted. "I replied that it is always difficult to find a quill when you need it. This way—" he patted the hat on his head "—I shall always have one close at hand."

"Oh, first-rate, sir," Vivian exclaimed.

"I hope you are happy that you've won your bet."

Rory clapped her hands. "Oh, is it done then? That is famous, Viv."

"Don't be so hasty," Vivian said. "It's true you've worn the hat. But no other gentleman—"

"I intercepted Clive scurrying about the Park looking for feathers on the ground. I assure you that within the hour he will have his version of Trawley's hat." His words were trenchant, but his eyes softened. "What favour shall you ask of Trawley?"

"Ten pounds."

"Ten pounds!" he ejaculated as Rory made a similar outcry.

"Vivian, you must be funning."

"I didn't go through all this fuss and botheration for a mere ten pounds," Reed said. "Do you understand that Trawley will grant you any favour your heart desires? He is not a pauper."

"I assure you that it is all I want."

Perplexed, he glanced at her heart-shaped face, at the dark eyes which usually brimmed with mischief. A blue satin ribbon from her chip hat fell against one of her dark ringlets, and he repressed the urge to twirl both round his finger.

Any other female by now would have been imagining herself in rubies and diamonds from Rundell's. Perhaps Miss Spalding did not realize the depth of Trawley's pockets.

"Trawley is very well pursed," he said now.

"Nevertheless, all I want from him is ten pounds. It's what I would have wagered. Unless..." She hesitated.

Reed relaxed. So she did have something else to importune Trawley for. All females possessed a streak of avarice.

"What is it? A diamond bracelet? A sapphire pendant?" he asked indulgently. "Rest easy. He can certainly afford one or the other."

"Mr. Reed, the very idea of my accepting such gifts! I would not accept them from *any* gentleman."

"I beg your pardon. Such selflessness is seldom seen in London. What favour would you have Trawley perform, then?"

She bit her lip. "Do you know Lady Jersey?"

His own lips twisted in a grimace. "Too well. A prattle-box if I've ever heard one. One wag calls her Silence because she so rarely is."

"I accidentally offended her."

Reed pushed back his feathered hat, intrigued by her comment. "A serious offence, Miss Spalding. How did this happen? Did your American exuberance get the better of you?"

"Yes, but it was partly your fault and Trawley's."

"Mine? I haven't seen Sally Jersey in at least a month, thank Jupiter."

"It was the day Trawley and I were discussing our wager and the feathered headband," Vivian explained. "Lady Jersey came calling on Rory's aunt. She was wearing a turban with a most enormous ostrich feather in it, longer than the one on your hat now. I took one look at it and—" She spread her hands helplessly.

"The two of you went into whoops of laughter," he said, unable to resist a chuckle himself. "A serious error."

Vivian heaved a sigh. "So I have become aware. I wrote and apologized immediately, but she hasn't answered me."

"She nurses her grudges," Reed said not unsympathetically. "But what has Lady Jersey to do with your request of Trawley?"

"I thought he might be induced to speak to her on my behalf."

Reed looked as though he had been struck dumb. "You want him to speak to Lady Jersey for you?" he croaked finally.

"Yes," she said innocently. "Do you think it is an unreasonable request?"

For a moment Reed was taken aback. He was the viscount's friend and, as such, loath to speak publicly of Trawley's rakish reputation. On the other hand Miss Spalding was a very green girl.

"If I were you, I'd as lief ask him for a bauble from Rundell the jeweller. Trawley would be better able to supply that request."

At that very moment Trawley himself appeared next to Reed, clapping one hand on his friend's shoulder.

"Ah, Lucian, the supreme arbiter of fashion."

"Will you stop calling me that?" Reed said, annoyed. "I am beginning to hate the expression."

"I beg your pardon. Who are you talking to in the carriage?" he asked, peering in. "Why, it's Miss Spalding and Miss Rory. Good day to you both."

"Good day," they answered.

"Miss Spalding, you have won the bet. I just saw two young sprigs bound for Locke's, ready to demand that he make them a hat similar to Reed's. If I were a peacock I would be afraid to go out in the street lest all my feathers be plucked by those aping Lucian's lead."

"Do spare my blushes," Reed said to his friend.

"I believe a sketch of you is going to appear in the *Gazette*. Mr. Kean could not have turned in a better performance." Trawley laughed again. "Now then, Miss Spalding, what favour may I grant you? Something along the lines of Rundell's best?"

"All I want is ten pounds."

Trawley looked shocked. "Ten pounds?"

"And for you to speak to Lady Jersey on my behalf," Vivian added, taking her fences in a rush.

The viscount exchanged speaking glances with Reed.

"I would so like to be able to go to Alma's," Vivian explained.

"Almack's!" Rory corrected. "Well, I don't. They serve only stale cakes."

"Yes, but Lady Edwina wishes it," her sister replied. "It is such a coil, my lord. Lady Jersey took umbrage at something we did."

"Not unusual. A high stickler."

"I thought perhaps if you would intercede on our behalf, tell her that you were a friend of ours..."

Trawley choked. "My dear Miss Spalding, what you ask would be impossible. Lady Jersey and I are not on good terms. If I spoke for you, she would become even more adamant against you."

Vivian's face fell.

"But you are a viscount," Rory said. "Vivian and I read a book that said viscounts were very important in English Society."

"That would depend on which viscount," Trawley replied. "I'm afraid disapproval follows this particular viscount. Ask Lucian. I am an ugly customer, am I not, Reed?"

"But why?" Rory asked.

"The details are not important," Reed interjected, thinking that perhaps he might speak to Sally Jersey privately. The Patroness was odiously starched up, but he might prevail on her to relent against the Spalding sisters. But it were best to keep his counsel to himself lest he raise hopes that might later be dashed down.

"Do you want something besides the ten pounds?" Trawley asked now.

Vivian shook her head. "No, thank you. The ten pounds will do."

The viscount opened his purse and counted out the money.

"Not a greedy woman," he observed later to Reed after the earl's carriage had gone off with the two Americans.

"No." Reed agreed. "Pity you couldn't help her with Sally Jersey."

Trawley grimaced. "You forget Sally was a fourth cousin to that Bradley chit." He paused. "Miss Spalding is a rarity, and I want to give her something more than ten pounds."

"Not diamonds or rubies. She made plain what she thought of females who accepted such trinkets from gentlemen."

"There must be something more I can do," Trawley said. He was still mulling over the situation as they parted company, and it was not until later that evening that he found an answer.

From Rory's chatter the day at the Zoo he knew that Vivian was troubled by the expenses of her new wardrobe. She had fought shy of accepting the earl's generosity. Perhaps a quiet word to Fanchon that he would be responsible for Miss Spalding's bills would be in order.

AT BRUTON STREET the next morning Vivian was staring at Rory and the very chic blue walking dress that Fanchon had sewn.

"Madame, you're a genius!"

The modiste, always glad to have confirmation of her genius, beamed.

"And what do you say about the dress you are wearing, Mademoiselle?" she asked.

Vivian turned her head to see her russet curls cascading down the back of her red walking dress. High-buttoned and high-collared, it was a dress that would attract notice and attention.

"I call it the Mandarin," Fanchon explained. "La Chinoise is all the rage here and the style suits you to perfection."

"I do not recall selecting red, Madame."

"It is not red," Fanchon contradicted. "Rose. A deep deep rose. Nearly a red," she conceded. "Red is very popular in China. Indeed, it is said to be a sign of good luck."

Vivian examined her reflection closely. She did like it. But would Londoners think her fast? She still hoped to make amends eventually with Lady Jersey and to be given entry into Almack's.

"What do you think, Rory?" Vivian enquired. "I do like it. But shall it make me look fast?"

"I think it looks dashing," her sister answered. "And if you don't want it, maybe Madame can make it over for me."

"It is a pity Lady Edwina is home with the grippe. I could have asked her opinion."

"Go with your heart, Mademoiselle," Fanchon advised. "Does it excite you? Please you?"

Vivian took another look at herself. "I'll take it," she said.

"Very good. And now you must try on your other dresses and your ball gowns."

Vivian went to change into the ball gowns, wondering if she would ever get a chance to attend a ball. After all, they were in Lady Jersey's black books.

Alerted by one of her girls that Viscount Trawley had requested a word with her, Fanchon left the back rooms.

As one who dressed the leaders of the ton, Fanchon was fully cognizant of Trawley's position in Society. She had no quarrel with him. He paid the bills for his chère amies promptly, unlike others she could mention. As she greeted him, she wondered idly which female was now enjoying his patronage.

"My lord, you favour us with your presence today."

"Madame Fanchon, you look as ravishing as any of the ladies you gown."

She laughed. "You have something in mind to order for a new friend?"

Trawley gave a rueful smile. "Alas, in matters of fashion I fall far behind my friend, Lucian Reed. It is on another matter that I come today. You are making a new wardrobe for Miss Spalding, I believe?"

"The American? *Oui.*"

"She is somewhat reluctant to have you bill her sister's grandfather."

Fanchon nodded. "Yes. Even now she is insisting that one ball gown will do instead of three. Yet she cannot appear in the same ball gown at all of the balls."

"I agree."

"But she will not hear of my sending a very large bill to the earl." Fanchon shrugged. "What can I do?"

"You can tell her that you will give her the three gowns for the price of one."

"*Sacrebleu!*"

"And send the bill for the two gowns to me."

Fanchon nodded, wise in the ways of the Quality she served.

"You understand?"

"I understand perfectly. Miss Spalding's bill for two ball gowns to be sent to you and not the earl."

"She is not to know of this!"

"No," Fanchon agreed. "My lips are sealed. I shall make all the arrangements."

After Trawley left, Fanchon gave the order to her chief clerk about the bills for Miss Spalding's gown, then went back to see how the Americans were doing.

Vivian was standing before the mirror, turning this way and that in a pale blue gown with a rather low neckline. She looked worried.

"You do not like it?" Fanchon asked.

"Oh, I love it. But it is a trifle daring, don't you think?"

"Mademoiselle, you do not know what daring is. Some females appear in dresses so thin that one can see everything, and even Caro Lamb herself donned damp petticoats."

"Good heavens, she would be sure to catch her death of cold."

"The grippe is just a little consequence of following the dictates of fashion," Fanchon pointed out. "If you appear in that gown the gentlemen are sure to be dangling after you."

"A pity Mr. Reed isn't here to tell us what he thinks," Rory said in her own gown of topaz silk and satin.

"Reed has promised me that he will never say a word about any dress of mine again," Vivian said. "I do like this blue. But then again, the rose one was very nice."

"You did not like the silver gown?" Fanchon asked. Of the three she had made for Miss Spalding, it was her own favourite.

"Oh, I love it. But I cannot really afford three gowns."

"Vivian, do stop being a goose. Grandfather said that he would pay for your wardrobe."

"That is not necessary. One ball gown is all that I will allow him to pay for."

"My clerk made an error when she quoted you the figure for the gowns, Miss Spalding," Fanchon said now. "The price she quoted was for all three, not for one apiece."

Vivian turned in astonishment. "But I thought you quoted me the price, Madame."

"I was relying on figures that she supplied," Fanchon lied smoothly. "So you see. You can have the three ball gowns for little more than the price of one."

"Oh, Vivian!" Rory exclaimed. "That's famous. Now we can be perfectly gowned for all our balls."

"Yes," Vivian said, wondering just which ball they would be attending. If they didn't mend their fences with Lady Jersey, the gowns would simply gather dust in their wardrobes.

"And can we wear our walking dresses out now?" Rory asked.

"*Bien sûr,*" Madame Fanchon replied.

While the Americans changed for the final time, Fanchon went out into the front of her shop to find Miss Astrid Long arguing with a seamstress about a garment she wished to have made.

"A dress with feathered what?" one of the seamstresses was asking.

"Sleeves," Astrid said. She caught sight of Fanchon. "Will you be able to make such a garment for me, Madame?"

"I can make anything," the modiste said with aplomb. "But I cannot guarantee that you would like it. Why do you wish to have sleeves made of feathers?"

Astrid paused, not wanting to have it known that she was following anyone's fashion lead, not even Lucian's.

"I have long had the idea. Will you do it?"

"Give me three days."

"Two."

"I will need to find the feathers," Fanchon said. "They may be expensive. Have you thought of that?"

"Are you dunning me?" Astrid demanded. Her rank as London's premier Beauty necessitated that she have a new dress for each occasion. Her father was indulgent but could be slow about paying tradesmen.

"*Non,*" Fanchon said immediately. "I merely point out such a dress would be expensive. My clerk will tell you just how much."

Fanchon's clerk, who was writing out the bills for the Spalding dresses, laid them aside to compute the cost of Miss Long's feathered dress. Astrid's impatient eyes swept over the crowded counter and saw the scribbled note the clerk had written to herself.

Vivian Spalding's two ball gowns to be paid by Viscount Trawley.

Astrid Long's nose twitched. Trawley was up to his old tricks again. How stupid for the American to fall for his easy charm. But then what could one expect of a colonial?

"Here is the cost of your feathered gown," the clerk said, presenting her with a bill.

Astrid's eyebrows lifted.

"There must be an error. This is far too much."

The clerk shook her head. "Madame said there will be extra work to attach the feathers, and then the price of the feathers themselves."

"Highway robbery," Astrid said.

"You are free to go to another modiste," the clerk said. Neither she nor her employer stood for any nonsense from their clients. Fanchon was the best. Everyone knew that.

Astrid swallowed her angry retort. It was worth any price to appear à la mode.

"Very well. I shall return on Thursday for the dress."

As she prepared to leave, she caught sight of two ladies emerging from the back room, one in a blue walking dress and the other in a deep rose. For a moment she was at a loss to place them, then the unmistakably American accents gave the pair away. The Spaldings were dressed in Fanchon's best and certain to turn heads.

Astrid felt her mood become grim. She had never given them a second thought when they were dressed like dowds, but now she eyed them with considerable misgiving. She had always thought her position as the most fashionable lady in London secure. Now she was no longer certain. She watched in mute fury as Fanchon herself hovered about the American pair.

But as she swept out the door she calmed herself. It was too absurd to think that country yokels could occupy the place she now possessed. Besides, she had certain information about Miss Spalding which would prevent anyone of good standing from even speaking to her. And an on-dit of such deliciousness was certainly too good to keep to herself.

CHAPTER SIX

AS THE DAYS PASSED Reed felt a twinge of regret over his role in bringing feathers to the attention of the fashionable world. Although he fully expected coxcombs like Clive to take their cue from him, he had not expected to extend a similar influence into the female quarter.

But after his first glance at the dress Astrid had commissioned from Fanchon and the hat presented to her by her milliner, he was very nearly undone.

"My dear Astrid, you cannot go out looking like that," he protested on Friday morning, with difficulty keeping his laughter at bay. The hat alone involved at least ten different varieties of fowl.

Miss Long was not pleased. She had been preening for several minutes in her bedchamber and had fully expected that Lucian would be in raptures. Mr. Clive had been when she told him about the garment she was commissioning.

"Has Clive seen the hat?" Reed quizzed doubtfully when this charge was put to him.

"I wore it for him yesterday, and he thought it superb. The variety of hues brought out the unique colour of my eyes."

"Wouldn't put too much credence in Clive's opinion. I always thought the fellow colour-blind myself. Has an appalling affinity for violet and scarlet neckcloths."

Astrid stamped her foot. "He is not colour-blind. You are just disagreeable, Lucian, because you have been eclipsed."

He laughed out loud then. "Eclipsed, my dear?"

"Yes," she sniffed. "Were we to go out together all eyes would be on me. You could not bear that."

"That would be unforgivable," he murmured.

"Tell the truth, Lucian. You are jealous."

Reed had had enough of her bibble-babble. "My dear Astrid, if the hat pleases you, wear it. I daresay I have endured enough talk about feathers to last a lifetime!"

Miss Long acknowledged this capitulation by linking her arm in his, an unfortunate move which caused the row of feathers on her hat to tickle his nose. Manfully he repressed the urge to sneeze as he led her to his carriage.

"You didn't tell me where we were driving to," she said, settling into his high perch phaeton.

"To Hookam's," he said, throwing back his multicaped driving cloak and picking up the reins. This excursion was the first in his campaign to prove that he and Astrid were more than bird-wits.

Although not a prodigious reader, he had enjoyed Mr. Scott's work, and word that a new book by that gentleman had appeared made him eager to buy it. He was certain that Astrid would find its merit as well. And if Mr. Scott proved too arduous for her, she might try the new novel *Sense and Sensibility,* which had received much praise.

However, Miss Long's aghast expression of horror soon made plain what she thought of Reed's destination.

"Do you mean that horrid bookshop?" she wailed. "Oh, Lucian. You must be funning. I would never have worn my hat if I'd known..."

"You can always remove it," he said, taking the corner with nary a pull on the rein.

Miss Long's retreat into silence expressed what she thought of *that* suggestion.

Reed's team of Welshbreds cantered on in the brisk May wind.

"Next week Mr. Humphrey Davy is lecturing on the properties of gas at an Open Day. Would you care to attend it with me?" he asked.

If Reed had suddenly commanded Astrid to jump into the Thames without any clothes on, she could not have appeared more shocked.

"On the properties of what?"

Reed's gloved hand tightened momentarily on the reins. "Gas."

"Lucian, I fear you are unhinged," said his companion. "Pray, don't speak a word more about such a ridiculous notion. You can't be serious." She fanned herself. "A lecture on gas, indeed. They might have a demonstration, and the fumes would wrinkle my dress."

"So they might," he agreed. Science definitely was not Astrid's strong suit.

He pulled the carriage to a halt in front of the store, and Miss Long descended, still displeased by their outing. Her frostiness disappeared when she discovered that several young ladies were present and each begged leave to compliment her on her hat.

"So original!"

"Thank you," she said, preening. "You see, Lucian," she told him in a whisper. "Your opinion is not shared by those of my sex."

Reed left her with her friends and moved down the aisle, attracted to a series of landscaping pamphlets on a table. He had always enjoyed helping Trawley with his plans for his country estate, and ofttimes indulged himself with the secret ambition of one day buying and refurbishing a country home of his own, to take the place of the family house lost due to his father's gaming.

Absorbed in thought, he moved towards the front of the store to purchase his pamphlets and the latest Scott. As he did so, he noticed the Spalding sisters browsing through the open shelves.

Fanchon had outdone herself with their walking dresses, he decided, as he raised his quizzing glass to admire Rory in a captivating sprig muslin and Vivian in a striking azure blue. As though they could feel his eyes on them, both ladies looked up.

"Mr. Reed!" Rory waved. "How do you like my dress?"

"First-rate," he said with obvious sincerity.

He turned towards her sister and bowed.

"And have you nothing to say about Vivian's dress?" Rory prompted.

His lip twitched. "Your sister and I have reached an agreement that I must never ever comment on her dress," he said.

Vivian laughed. "I should like nonetheless to know what you think of this one."

He wagged his finger playfully at her. "None of your tricks, Miss Spalding. I have been scorched before. A promise is a promise."

"You are most vexatious," she said. "And I am surprised to see you here at Hookam's."

"What do you have there?" Rory demanded. "Oh, just some dreary old pamphlets on landscape and furniture."

"Furniture?" Vivian asked. "Mr. Chippendale's work?"

"Yes," he replied, as she browsed through one of the booklets. "You know the name then?"

"Even in America we have heard of Mr. Chippendale, and Mr. Capability Brown and Mr. Inigo Jones."

"And what are you purchasing?" he asked, taking advantage of his height to peer over her head.

"A new book by the author of *Pride and Prejudice*," Vivian said. "We so enjoyed the story of the Bennett girls that we are hopeful this one will be just as good."

"And I have a new romance," Rory put in. "I do so love the parts when the hero sweeps the heroine off on his horse. It's so dashing."

"Is it really? Remind me not to take you riding," he put in, and the three of them began to laugh.

"Lucian?" a querulous voice asked. They turned to find Astrid striding up the aisle.

The sight of the Beauty's hat caused a tickle in Vivian's throat, a tickle which threatened to consume her. Still, her earlier mishap with Lady Jersey had brought home the fact that one must never ever laugh at another woman's hat, no matter what the circumstances.

One look at Rory, however, and she knew that her sister had not learned anything from the Lady Jersey débâcle. And lest they disgrace themselves yet again, she hastily thrust her books back on the table.

"We shall purchase these another time. Come, Rory. Quickly!" She attempted to drag her out the door.

But her sister would not be hurried. Instead Rory turned to Miss Long, greeting her in her friendly way.

"Oh Miss Long, do you have a wager afoot, too? I vow, it is the silliest hat I have ever seen! Even worse than Mr. Reed's, and that took Lord Trawley nearly a day to fashion! Who is your wager with?"

"Wager? What is all this prattle?" Astrid demanded in an outraged tone.

"Haven't you told her?" Vivian asked Reed in an urgent whisper.

"No," he murmured, fortifying himself with a pinch of snuff. He did not relish the scene unfolding in front of his helpless eyes. What was it about the Spalding sisters which made even the most ordinary encounter with them a scene worthy of Mrs. Siddons?

"What wager is this?" Miss Long asked again.

"Reed's, of course," Rory replied.

"You are out of your head. Reed never wagers on anything. You would know this if you were in the swim of things here in London."

Rory took the insult without a blink. "It wasn't *his* wager, but Vivian and Trawley's. The bet was that if he wore a feathered hat in London it would soon become all the rage with the gentlemen."

Astrid's head swivelled in Reed's direction.

"Is this true?" she hissed.

"Yes," he acknowledged. "I had no notion that you would adopt the fashion, and in point of fact I gave you my opinion of your hat earlier today."

The justice in his statement in no way assuaged her anger. Miss Long snatched off her hat and threw it onto the floor, then marched straight out of the store and summoned a hack to take her back to Cavendish Square.

"Heavens, now you've done the thing," Reed murmured.

"Rory said nothing that was out of the way," Vivian replied. "You are to blame for your own difficulty. You should not have let her out on the street dressed in that silly hat." She lifted her chin defiantly. "And it *was* silly."

"You should have told her about the wager," Rory added.

He glanced from one face to the other, amused in spite of himself at being issued a set-down by a pair of American brats.

He flicked a speck of dust from his driving cape. "I did tell her the hat didn't suit her. She didn't believe me."

Vivian's dark eyes sparkled with amusement. "I shan't believe that! So supreme an arbiter of fashion as Lucian Reed..."

"Will you stop calling me that!" he beseeched. "I have never felt less like a supreme arbiter since the day I met the two of you," he added, with a frankness that surprised them. "Besides, I couldn't really tell Astrid she looked like a cake in the hat. She would take it as an insult. I am not in the habit of insulting ladies."

"You insulted me," Vivian reminded him.

"Not deliberately," he pointed out. "Astrid is different. She is very conscious of her position and rank here in London, while you—"

"I am just an American nobody?" she quizzed. A dangerous glint replaced the amusement in her eyes.

"I was going to say that you do not appear conscious of your position or rank here."

"That is because I have none. My father is an American."

He cocked his head at her. "Don't be a peagoose. Do you think the Earl of Atwater would allow his daughter, Lady Pamela, to wed just anyone? Your father's people had rank, or I'll go bail."

She had never thought of her father's second marriage in that light. Her father had never volunteered much in the way of family history.

"So you needn't bring up your American heritage in every conversation with me," he said with a smile.

"It seems that there are some who consider my American heritage the ultimate in insults, sir."

"Then you should remind them that while England did vanquish Napoleon, she had no such victory over America. Indeed, of the two wars fought between England and America, America won both," he said gently.

THE ENSUING COLDNESS between Astrid Long and Lucian Reed did not pass unnoticed in London circles. Astrid had too much pride to make known what had happened, but others present that morning at Hookam's repeated with great relish what had been said. Before the sun set all of Society had divided itself into two camps.

Surprisingly, the majority of ladies sided with Miss Long. Although Astrid was not of a friendly nature and her toplofty manners were at times difficult to tolerate, she was still a prime favourite of the Patronesses.

"I have always had a fondness for Reed, but he should not have made her the butt of his joke," Lady Jersey remarked privately to her fellow Patronesses.

"It wasn't just Reed," Countess Lieven said, her expressive eyes giving a playful archness to her words. "I have heard that Trawley had some part to play in this whole shabby affair."

"And the Americans," Mrs. Drummond Burrell added.

"But surely not Lady Edwina's niece," Lady Sefton said fretfully. "Edwina is such a pet."

"Too charitable, as usual." The Princess Esterhazy looked bored as she surveyed the other Patronesses seated in the Jersey drawingroom. "I have heard it said that the elder Miss Spalding is Trawley's latest chère amie. Fanchon dresses her and sends the bill to him."

Mrs. Drummond Burrell was nothing if not a stern moralist. "That settles that. No vouchers. Not now—or ever."

Nods of agreement answered her words.

"We'll give them the cut direct," Lady Jersey said. "Won't recognize them in the street. They'll get the message soon enough."

"What about Lady Edwina?" Lady Sefton protested, continuing to worry about her old friend.

"Oh, we shall continue to recognize Edwina," the countess assured her. "But the Americans will discover that we in London are not objects to be laughed at."

UNAWARE OF THE PUNISHMENT about to be meted out to him and the Spaldings, Reed spent an exasperated evening at White's. His quarrel with Astrid had followed him to the club, with the bay window set wanting to know more about his joke on her.

"Devil take it, the joke wasn't supposed to be on her!" Reed expostulated. "And if she had a modicum of sense, this affair would never have arisen."

"I saw her in the hat," Lord Tolmaine snickered. "Almost thought a chicken was roosting in her hair!"

"Well, at least we know that you're not daft, Lucian," Mr. Harrow said when the laughter ceased. "When I saw you in the Park wearing that concoction, I thought you had taken leave of your senses."

More laughter greeted this remark, and after a few glasses of claret, Reed discovered that the majority of the gentlemen were stoutly on his side, with the exception of Mr. Clive, who felt humiliated in his new feathered hat.

"Do you plan on healing the breach with Astrid?" someone asked.

"I shall apologize tomorrow."

HOWEVER, ASTRID DID NOT want Reed's apology. He called twice and was refused entrance at her residence in Cavendish Square. His note to her, delivered by his footman, was returned in tiny pieces.

"She must have taken scissors to them!" Trawley said, examining them under his quizzing glass. "Look at how tiny they are and so perfectly straight!"

"Did she read it, then?" Reed questioned his servant.

"No, sir. She cut up the note and bade me fling the remnants into your face."

"Devil, she's not even giving me the chance to apologize."

"Apologize for what?" Trawley enquired. He had been out of London for the past twenty-four hours.

Learning what had transpired in his absence, he threw back his head and roared with laughter.

"By Jove, I would give a pony to have seen her in that hat at Hookam's."

Reed poured himself a glass of Madeira. "This is all your fault, George. Yours and the Spaldings for that stupid bet. It was your idea. Now think how I can get out of Astrid's black books."

"I don't think you can, Lucian," Trawley said, sipping his Madeira. "She is having too much fun being the wounded party. I know that type of female only too well," he said, looking grim.

"There must be something I may do."

"Send her a trinket from Rundell's. That generally does the trick."

"What an excellent notion!" Reed agreed.

However, even the bauble from Rundell's failed to end the breach with Astrid. Miss Long did waver somewhat at the sight of the exquisite sapphire bracelet and even tried it on her wrist. But in the end she sent it back to Reed, an action which confirmed that the matter was more serious than anyone had thought.

JUST HOW SERIOUS the affair was became evident to the principals during the following week. On Monday the Spaldings accompanied Lady Edwina on a round of visits to her many London acquaintances. She was warmly received, but she was forced to admit that her hostesses seemed bent on ignoring Vivian and Rory. Since she was not one to think ill of anyone, she came to believe that the difference in age made it difficult for them to converse with her young guests.

Vivian had been on the receiving end of bad manners before, but she had not encountered so systematic a plot. On Tuesday when she and Rory went to the glovers, the shop instantly emptied, and the same thing happened when they went to Miss Starke, the milliner.

"Something is amiss," she said to Rory. "Everyone seems to be avoiding us."

"Perhaps it's because we're no longer the dowdy Americans?" Rory said optimistically.

"Lady Edwina usually has a score of callers on Tuesday. No one has called. That must mean something."

"What it means is that we are being given the cut direct," Lady Edwina informed her when Vivian returned to Hill Street and found her in bed with a tray of her favourite medicines close by. "I know the signs well."

"But why?"

Lady Edwina shrugged and adjusted her shawl about her thin shoulders. "Who is to say? The Patronesses's whims are notorious. Once they took a dislike to some chap who had the misfortune to wear a torn neckcloth to the Assembly. He was never allowed entry to any respectable drawingroom again. And they even denied entrance to Wellington because he came after the eleven o'clock hour."

Vivian was amazed that anyone would deny the hero of Waterloo anything.

"Your London ways are strange," she said.

Lady Edwina attempted a smile. "So I sometimes think myself. Ostracism is not easy to bear. Only think of Brummell himself. He was ostracized after his breach with Prinny."

REED'S FIRST INTIMATION that things were not as they should be occurred during one of his morning visits to Weston. As was his usual custom afterward he walked down Bond Street, where he encountered Lady Sefton and her maid. Tipping his hat at the Patroness, he directed his most winning smile her way.

"Good morning."

Lady Sefton stared off to the right.

"Lovely weather, isn't it?" he went on, wondering if she could be going deaf.

When she ventured no reply to this or to the other attempts at conversation he made, he could only conclude that she was queer in the attic. But when, the next day, he encountered Lady Jersey riding in the Park and attempted to rein in and speak with her, she set her Welshbreds off at a trot, leaving him with the unmistakable impression that his presence was not desired.

Trawley's reputation had caused most gently bred females to shun any possible contact with him, so at first he did not feel the full weight of the Patronesses's edict. But even he was forced to admit that something was in the wind when his charming sallies to the Countess Lieven, who had a soft spot in her heart for rakes, earned him not a crinkle of a smile.

"Something's in the wind," he told Reed that afternoon at White's.

"I know. I am being treated as though I had the plague."

"Not quite the plague," Mr. Clive, who chanced to overhear, said with a chuckle.

Reed turned a severe eye his way. "You know something, don't you? What is it? Out with it!" He shook his Malacca cane.

In the face of threatened violence, even of the nominal sort, Mr. Clive turned cat in the pan. "It is an order from the Patronesses. No female who wants a chance at the Marriage Mart can say a word to either of you or to your friends, the Spaldings."

"And what has earned us this contemptible treatment?" Reed enquired icily.

"It can't just be because of the hat!" Trawley said.

Mr. Clive flushed, recalling the specimen he himself had worn not a week before.

"From your antics it is plain that you two think yourselves above the normal strata of Polite Society, which you have embarrassed. Well, you're not above Society. Any female who speaks to you risks censure. The Patronesses have spoken."

A muscle worked in Reed's jaw. "Have they, indeed?" he said in a dangerous tone. "We shall see about that."

"It is a nuisance, I grant you," the viscount said, following Reed as he descended the stairs of the club. "But it shall blow over."

"I have done nothing to be treated in this way," Reed said, jabbing his cane at the loose cobble-stones in the street.

"Neither have I," Trawley avowed, keeping pace with him up St. James's Street. "I've never told you the truth about that Bradley chit, have I?" He looked over at his friend. "And you've never asked."

Reed dodged an errant coachman at the reins of a closed carriage. "Had no business asking."

"The truth is Anne Bradley came upon me in the inn and threw herself at me. I thrust her off, but she was already compromised and demanded I marry her. Well, I couldn't see myself marrying such a silly-headed chit. I refused to do the honourable thing, got branded a blackguard and she received all the sympathy."

"I didn't know that."

He shrugged. "One grows accustomed to being a blackguard in time, and I don't mind what they say about me. But I'll be dashed if I shall sit quietly and let them ruin the Spaldings."

"Nor shall I," Reed said with a vehemence that surprised even himself. "Let's go over and find out how they are coping with this impossible situation."

CHAPTER SEVEN

THE TWO GENTLEMEN upon calling at Hill Street, found Lady Edwina indisposed, and the earl enduring another painful episode with the gout. The Spalding sisters were practising at the pianoforte in the music room, but eagerly quit the keyboard to talk with their visitors.

Vivian had to admit that it was enjoyable to see friendly faces instead of the usual stony ones turned her way. Being snubbed by London Society was daunting to her spirit.

"Lady Edwina will be sorry to have missed you. We have been experiencing fewer and fewer callers of late."

Reed stripped off his York tan gloves and peered more closely at Vivian, noting the wan expression about her eyes.

"I see by your face that you have been subjected to the same abominable treatment we have. It is for that reason we have called."

"Do you mean to say I look hagged?" she enquired.

"What? I didn't mean..." Then he recognized her mischievous expression.

"Minx!"

"We shall all look hagged if we don't do something about this stupid incident," Trawley said with his usual good humour.

"How can they treat us so shabbily?" Rory asked.

"Easily, but rest assured we shall find a way out of the briars," Reed said.

"Perhaps some refreshment will help us devise a scheme," Vivian suggested and led them into the blue drawingroom. Over glasses of sherry for the gentlemen and lemonade for the ladies they began to discuss the problem, each one offering a solution that was hastily rejected by the other three.

"Now, the way I see it," said Reed, "we are being given what some might call the cut direct!"

"If that means no one will speak to us, that is what has been happening," Rory observed, nibbling on a biscuit. "Do you think it will go on much longer? No one speaking to us, I mean?"

"I have heard of some religious sects that may on occasion do that—shun those members whom they consider to be sinful," Vivian said, her fingers lightly tracing the pattern on the cut-crystal glass.

"Lud, I have a score of sins," Trawley exclaimed, "but I wouldn't call Almack's a religious sect, would you, Lucian?"

Reed shook his head. "No, although the Patronesses sometimes act like high priestesses of Society. Pity they aren't men; I'd challenge them to a duel and have done with it."

Vivian lifted a delicately arched eyebrow. "You do not strike me as the duelling sort, sir."

"Oh, Lucian handles a foil and a pistol as well as any other man," the viscount said. "And in his salad days he wasn't above meeting at dawn at Paddington Green to settle a score."

"But that must have been years ago..." Rory laid such emphasis on her words that Vivian choked down a laugh and Reed wondered why he should suddenly feel like Methuselah.

"So it was," Trawley said, casting a derisive eye at his friend. "And just which Patroness would you challenge, Reed? Do you see Sally Jersey as your opponent? No, I for one quite prefer Mrs. Burrell in the role."

The three of them laughed.

"Now, I feel better," Vivian said. "We can't just sit around here wringing our hands."

"We needn't sit anywhere in London," Rory pointed out. "Grandfather was saying only last week that we could be removing to the country shortly. We should go now instead of later."

"An excellent notion," Trawley agreed. "I was planning to oversee the refurbishment of my family house. You saw my plans and can come with me, Reed."

The peaceful countryside and the restoration of the house were tempting, but Reed shook his dark head firmly.

"The Patronesses will think they've won," he said, putting down his sherry. "I won't leave London until they apologize to us."

"Good heavens, then you are doomed to endure a sweltering summer," Trawley said mournfully.

"Asking the Patronesses to apologize is doing it too brown, sir," Vivian said. "Perhaps if we went together, the four of us, to the Patronesses and presented our side, as a united front."

"Like your United States?" Reed asked, quizzingly.

Before she could rise to this bait the viscount voiced his own objections to her plan.

"They won't listen," he said. "I tried that once some years ago on a minor matter." His lips curled at the memory. "Besides, nothing would please them more than to reject us out of hand. And we don't want them to think they have discomfited us."

"But they have!" Rory pointed out naïvely. "It is disagreeable to be treated like a toad. And even more disagreeable to pretend that it doesn't matter. Poor Aunt Edwina, I don't think she wants to show her face anywhere. And since she is prone to quack herself, I fear she may go into a decline."

Reed rose and paced the length of the room, nearly crashing into a Chinese lacquered screen. "What we must do is to plan some method of attack."

"Oh, yes, first-rate, Lucian. Go on," Trawley said encouragingly.

"That's all I have at the moment," Reed admitted, running his fingers through his dark hair.

"We need a strategy. That was the way Wellington outfoxed Napoleon," Trawley said.

Reed jabbed a finger at the golden dragon painted on the Chinese screen. "A direct attack. Beard the lionesses in their den."

"Do you mean Almack's?"

"Why not? If we appeared next Wednesday, that would challenge them to their faces."

"Agreed, but—"

"They would pull themselves together and turn you the cold shoulder," Vivian finished for Trawley. "And if the others go along with them, as they probably will since the majority of ladies there are little more than schoolroom misses, the Patronesses will have won the battle. Besides, Rory and I haven't vouchers for Almack's, so we could not be there to assist you in the attack."

"I think my scheme will work," Reed said. "Do you have any others of your own?"

"Well, no," she acknowledged. "But do just think for a moment. Storming Almack's may sound like good strategy, and I quite agree that we must bring the fight to the Patronesses, since they saw fit to issue this ridiculous order. But Almack's is their territory, and they have the advantage there!"

"There's logic to that, Lucian," Trawley observed.

"Well, if we can't storm Almack's, what *can* we do?" his friend enquired frostily.

Vivian chewed for a moment on a biscuit. "What do the gentlemen at White's think of the treatment that is being dished out to the two of you?"

Reed's lip curled. "They think it capital sport."

"All of them?"

"The tulips and the pinks."

"And the others with more rank and position, what do they say?"

The two men frowned, considering the matter.

"Davenport stopped me in the street and said that he for one didn't like it." The viscount turned to Vivian. "But what does that have to do with stopping the Patronesses?"

"What makes the Patronesses so powerful?" Vivian asked.

Reed snorted. "Almack's."

"And why is Almack's so popular? It cannot be the refreshments, which you have stigmatized as stale cakes and sour lemonade."

"Almack's is the Marriage Mart."

"Exactly!" Vivian nodded as though to a child who had suddenly got the right answer. "And why is it called that?"

"My dear Miss Spalding, your barrage of tedious questions is quite exhausting to me."

She ignored Reed and turned to Trawley. "Why is it called the Marriage Mart, my lord?"

The viscount's brow wrinkled. "Because that is the place where any matron with a daughter of marriage age brings her during the Season."

"Why?"

Trawley lifted his brow. "My dear Miss Spalding..."

"In order to see and be seen," Reed said, watching the gleam in her eyes. What were all her questions leading to?

"By whom?" Vivian continued. "The Patronesses? They aren't going to marry her, are they? The marriage-minded mamas bring their daughters to be seen by gentlemen such as yourselves, do they not?"

The two gentlemen exchanged glances. "Yes," Reed said, a glimmer of an idea beginning to form in his own brain.

"Without gentlemen at Almack's, the ladies can stand there looking beautiful for all Eternity, and no one would care a jot, would they?"

"No, by Jove!" Trawley chortled and slapped one fist into the palm of the other hand. "Keep the gentlemen away from the Marriage Mart. It's the perfect solution, don't you think, Lucian?"

"Miss Spalding, you are a genius," Reed announced.

"Thank you," she replied, feeling a thrill of pleasure at his compliment. "We must rely on the two of you to bring the scheme to fruition. Do you have enough friends who will assist you in this matter?"

"Leave it to us," Reed said with a chuckle. "Half the gentlemen don't wish to be at Almack's anyway," he said. And the discussion among the four of them began in earnest.

A CAMPAIGN TO KEEP ALL the gentlemen from Almack's would be futile, they had realized immediately. But all that was really necessary was that the most eligible gentlemen refrain from appearing. Reed and Trawley repaired to the viscount's establishment for the remainder of the day, compiling a list of the eligibles known to frequent Almack's.

High on that list stood the Marquis of Ludwin and the young, dashing Earl of Rutland, whose rank made them the target of many cap-setting females.

By the time the list was complete they had two dozen prime specimens and a dozen of the lesser rank.

"I think we should concentrate on the top twenty-four," Reed said, yawning and stretching in the viscount's book room.

"Seems a paltry number, two dozen," Trawley said fretfully. "A mere twenty-four."

"Twenty-six, if we count ourselves," Reed pointed out.

"Which we must. I wonder what Miss Spalding will think of the list."

Reed sipped the Madeira in front of him. "You seem to be taking an inordinate interest in Miss Spalding, George. Are you aware that the quizzes say she is the object of your gallantry?"

The viscount frowned.

"What are you prattling about? I've heard nothing."

"To be frank, there are those under the impression that she is your mistress."

Trawley slammed his fist down on the desk. "Who has uttered such vile slander?"

"I had the word from Clive," Reed replied.

Trawley rose from behind his mahogany desk. "And you take that coxcomb's word over mine?"

"Not at all. I bring it up simply to make you aware that the story is circulating. She was seen at Fanchon's with you, I believe. And the payment of her bill was ascribed—falsely, I know—to you!"

"Oh, blast! Fanchon promised—"

Reed's slate eyes narrowed. "So it's true?"

"Take a damper. It's not what you think. My taste runs to blondes, not independent-minded brunettes. I merely wished to give Miss Spalding something more than ten pounds. Rory had told me that Vivian did not want to be beholden to the earl for any of her wardrobe expenses, but the two were unaware of just how high prices would be. So I told Fanchon to send the earl a bill for one gown and send me the bill for the other two."

"That's all that it is? A payment on the wager?" Reed enquired.

"Yes."

"Good," Reed said, feeling curiously relieved. "Let's just hope Vivian has not heard the gossip-mongers."

THE FOLLOWING DAY he presented their list of eligible gentlemen to Vivian.

It was a very short list, Vivian saw with some dismay, and she knew hardly anyone on it. She would have to trust Reed was correct that these gentlemen constituted the top of the ton.

"If these gentlemen are the cream of the crop that's all we need. The Patronesses will definitely feel their absence," she said.

"As will the young ladies out to lure them to St. George's," Reed said.

"A harsh indictment of my sex, sir."

"You would quarrel with it?" he asked, flicking open his Sèvres snuff-box with his thumb-nail.

Her eyes danced. "No. I believe that no gentleman willingly sets foot in parson's mousetrap, except you, perhaps...."

"I?" He stood with a pinch of snuff between two fingers, looking shocked.

"Or do you mean to tell me that your engagement to Miss Long was coercion on her part?"

A smile lifted Reed's lips. "Touché, Miss Spalding." He inhaled the snuff. "And in actual fact I am not engaged to Miss Long; we have merely come to an understanding."

"Is there a difference?"

"Certainly. It's all the difference between being married and not being married. But enough about Astrid. If the list meets with your approval, then George and I shall set to work on eliciting the cooperation of these eligibles."

Miss Spalding readily gave her consent to the list, whereupon Reed and Trawley endeavoured to cross the paths of each man on the list. Reed had always been one of the more popular gentlemen of the ton, and the viscount was generally regarded as a fellow who gave no one except the ladies any trouble. At Watier's his play and his cheerful payment of his losses earned him the good will of many.

Most of the eligible gentlemen had felt the sting of the Patronesses' lash themselves, and the idea of serving them with their own sauce tickled their fancy.

"We'll bring the Marriage Mart to a halt!" Trawley chortled.

"Getting them to agree to stay away from Almack's Wednesday evening is one thing," Reed replied. "But what would really clinch the matter is if they were all gathered with us that evening having a merry old time."

"I shan't argue with that. But what sort of merriment do you have in mind?"

"Gentlemen usually have two things in mind when it comes to entertainments—sport and cards."

"They could gamble at Watier's or White's."

"Then it shall have to be sport."

"Easier said than done. Exactly what kind of sport can we indulge in under your roof?" Trawley demanded. "Wrestling, boxing, archery, shooting, fencing? All would do inestimable damage to one's residence."

"There must be something," Reed insisted. "Of course we could hold a shooting match out of doors."

"Not at night; wouldn't be fair. Boxing's a great attraction, but it would have to be on the heath."

"I have it!" Reed snapped his fingers. "There won't be any necessity to redo either of our Town residences. And it will keep the gentlemen so occupied that none of them will even think of Almack's."

THE NEXT MORNING footmen scurried to deliver invitations to twenty-four gentlemen to participate in a series of billiard matches to be held Wednesday evenings at Reed's residence.

Lord Rutland, who prided himself on his skill with a cue stick, was the first to reply in the affirmative, and the others soon followed suit.

The gentlemen buzzed of nothing but the tournament, with some cancelling all engagements to practise for the grand event. In addition to the twenty-four gentlemen invited to participate, another ten were called upon to assist in the judging of the game. Those who had not been invited to participate or judge the event were still welcome to view the matches. The tournament would commence at eight, and through an elimination format would probably come to an end sometime after midnight.

"And the prize?" Ludwin asked Reed when they met at the usual hour at Manton's shooting gallery.

Reed coolly aimed and fired at the target.

"The prize is the honour of being the best billiard player in London!" he replied once the bull's-eye had been confirmed. "Won't that be enough?"

"Oh, to be sure. The best billiard player in London." He flashed his engaging grin. "I like the sound of that, Reed."

Word of the billiard match reached Vivian courtesy of Lord Atwater, who had been swallowing Lady Edwina's tonic with a minimum of complaint each morning.

"Have to be better by Wednesday," he told Vivian. "I'm judging a billiard match at Reed's."

"Billiards, my lord?"

"Yes. It's quite respectable, my dear," he said hastily. "Talk of the Town, really, a match to prove who is the best billiard player in London."

"But a billiard match! That's not fair," Vivian protested when Reed called to inform her of their progress against the Patronesses.

"What's not fair about it?" Reed asked, admiring despite himself the charming picture she made in a sea-water green morning dress. The colour brought out the reddish glints in her hair.

"Rory and I wanted to view the proceedings. How can we, if it is a stupid billiard match?"

"I know it is a trifle disappointing," Reed said. "But that was the only scheme we could devise."

"How would you feel if we agreed on a plan and put it to work without letting you view the outcome?"

"I'm sorry, Miss Spalding. Disappointed or not, you cannot possibly attend the billiard match. The invitations are sent to gentlemen only. And isn't the main thing to beat the Patronesses at their own game?"

Mollified by this reminder that their enemy was the Patronesses and not each other, Vivian fell silent, but ideas churned in her brain. She would be dashed if she would sit quietly on the sidelines while the gentlemen enjoyed themselves!

ALMACK'S ASSEMBLY ROOMS in King Street were not the largest to be found in London nor the most ornate. They were simple, almost deplorably plain, but as a rule no one noticed because of the bevy of beauties dancing to the music with the handsome swallow-tailed gentlemen.

The musicians, valiantly playing, were in attendance this evening along with the lovely young ladies in their best gowns and smiles, but the gentlemen were not. The few males who climbed the staircase were tulips like Mr. Clive who had an acknowledged place in Society, but there was not one who could hold a candle to Ludwin or Rutland.

Miss Peabody, who had been trying to land the marquis, was particularly hard pressed not to burst into tears over his absence as she circulated about the empty ballroom. She had stood up with Clive because he had asked her, but she did not wish to do so again even if he were only one of a handful of men. She found his prattle gave her the headache.

Astrid Long knew better than to appear at Almack's too early, so when she made her arrival it was nearly ten o'clock. Great was her astonishment to find that most of the couples had given up all pretence of dancing and had taken what solace could be found in the refreshment room.

Several red-faced matrons who had squandered vast sums on their daughters' ball dresses could be seen choking on the stale cakes as they mentally computed the monies wasted.

Since she had dressed herself with particular care that evening, Astrid, too, was annoyed to find that the only one who fully appreciated her dress was Clive, and that even his comments were delivered in a somewhat distracted vein.

"Almack's is rather thin of company tonight," she observed as they danced. Usually it was all but impossible to dance without bumping into another couple, but they had the ballroom practically to themselves.

"Very thin," Mr. Clive tittered. In the absence of other gentlemen of rank, he had been dancing with some of the prime Beauties and now seemed to treat Astrid in a rather offhand manner.

This did not set well in her dish, and after the quadrille ended, she went off to find Lady Jersey and discover what was amiss.

"I should have stayed home rather than be seen standing about like a wallflower," she overheard one Beauty lament.

"Once one begins to be seen lacking for partners, it leads to the most disagreeable rumours," another agreed.

"Where is everyone?" Astrid asked Lady Jersey, who was making a brave attempt at gaiety. The Patroness frowned, in no way pleased that Astrid should be so bold about making obvious the defects of the Assembly that evening. Far better to pretend to be having a good time than to admit that the ball was a failure.

"If you mean the other Patronesses, most were not able to attend this evening," Lady Jersey said in a casual manner that fooled no one.

"I am not speaking of them. Where are the gentlemen?"

Lady Jersey eyed Astrid with some dislike. She had never been fond of the creature, finding her vain and wilful, even if she wore clothes to perfection. Their feathered hats had given them a bond, but that was dwindling daily, particularly when Lady Jersey had occasion to remember that she enjoyed speaking with Reed more than she did Astrid.

"I don't know," Lady Jersey said coldly now as Astrid repeated her question of where the gentlemen could be. "Now, pray excuse me, I must speak to Maria Sefton."

The two Patronesses stood, chattering away, continuing to hope that the gentlemen would be making a belated appearance. They even toyed fleetingly with the notion of, just for the evening, not enforcing the eleven o'clock rule, if perchance some gentlemen should appear after that hour. Wellington had arrived to a full room, but the one this evening was only a quarter full.

But when eleven o'clock came no gentlemen hurried down the stairs.

In the refreshment room Astrid was standing in a corner, plying Mr. Clive with food in a vain attempt to keep him at her side.

Mr. Clive was feeling quite light-headed, having enjoyed the unaccustomed pleasure of the company of not one Beauty but a half dozen. He had danced with more females than usually accepted his compliments, and it was a novelty to have his attention solicited, by one or the other. The glasses of champagne he had drunk, too, made him more than a little light-headed.

"Mr. Clive, do you happen to know where Lord Ludwin is?" Miss Peabody asked, looking anxious.

"Or Lord Rutland?" asked another lady.

Mr. Clive puffed up his cheeks, pleased to show that he was a source of considerable information. "Certainly I know. They're at Lucian Reed's establishment."

"What are they doing there?"

"He has sponsored a billiard match for this evening. Invited all those who would ordinarily come here. Paying the Patronesses back for dealing them a snub." He fell silent, becoming aware that the ladies present included Lady Jersey and Lady Sefton.

"Mr. Clive, pray repeat that," Lady Jersey boomed. "Did we hear you say that Reed is paying us back for dealing him a snub?"

"Yes. Trawley is part of this scheme as well. And the Spalding sisters, the Americans. Battle of the Wednesdays, they are calling it over at White's. But I don't need to tell you who won tonight's battle," he said naïvely. "Capital ball, don't you think?"

Lady Jersey subscribed to the theory of slaying the bearer of bad news and emptied a glass of champagne directly over Mr. Clive's head.

CHAPTER EIGHT

"POINT AND MATCH to Ludwin!" Reed announced as the crowd of men clustered about the billiard table let out a roar.

"Well done!" Lord Rutland wiped his brow and thrust out his palm at his opponent. The two had been locked in a breathless battle most of the night.

"That brings you to the semifinals next week, Nigel," Trawley said, making some fast computations. "Your opponent will be whoever wins the last match in the blue saloon."

Hearing that, Ludwin and his cronies, including the just vanquished Rutland, swept out to the blue saloon, where the final match of the evening was being contested.

In the now empty billiard room Reed poured two glasses of claret and handed one to Trawley.

"A fine turn-out, George. If there's a sprig worth anything at Almack's this evening I'll eat my beaver hat."

"With or without feathers?" the viscount drawled.

Reed threw back his head and laughed. "It is gratifying to know that one can still pull off a game like this."

"Even Moreton is here, and he has been dangling after that Fortescue chit half the Season. Quite an accomplishment to snare him."

"He is partial to the cue," Reed explained. "It was a very good thing that I had the foresight to pit him against George Henderson for an easy win. That means he advances to next week's match."

"How long do you think we will be able to keep this going?" Trawley asked.

"As long as necessary."

"And after the billiard champion is crowned?"

Reed shrugged and held the crystal glass of claret up to the light. The dark liquid reminded him of the colour of Miss Spalding's hair.

"Then we go on to some other sport," he said. "Such as archery, boxing, shooting. By then we'll have engaged the gentlemen's attention long enough that I believe we could adjourn to some outside area without worrying that they shall stray back to Almack's."

The viscount eyed him carefully. "You are taking this personally, Lucian."

"I do not enjoy being snubbed unjustly." It reminded Reed of his childhood, when others had laughed at him behind his back for his father's predicament. He shook off the memory. "Come on... let's see what is happening in the other match."

He led Trawley into the blue saloon, where Sir Alec Minton was just managing to nudge his opponent's ball into a precarious position. The move occasioned shouts of approval among the onlookers.

As he leaned his lanky frame against the doorway, Reed counted the heads in the room. At least fifty. Twenty-four of them were participants. The others were guests or those who had heard about the match and begged leave to watch. He cast his gaze at two callow-looking youths on the couch. It seemed that University lads had got wind of the match, too.

He strolled over towards the pair, who were garbed in the most antiquated coats imaginable, no doubt all the rage at the University. Neither neckcloth was known to Reed, but he forgave them this transgression as he recalled various hasty and ill-knotted creations of his own salad days.

"Enjoying the matches, lads?" he asked.

The pair started. There was not even a trace of down on their faces, he noticed.

"Er, yes...sir, very much," one of them, with blue eyes, piped up.

His voice hadn't even deepened.

"Do you play?" he enquired, sitting down next to them.

"No!" the one on his right intoned.

"Yes!" said the one on his left.

They exchanged glances and fell silent.

"So you—" he turned to the blue-eyed boy "—play and you—" he smiled at the other "—do not. In either case you are welcome. I remember the problem of University dining, so I take leave to say that you should partake of the refreshments while they last."

"Thank you, sir! Very kind of you, sir."

Reed strolled off, leaving a relieved pair on the couch. The two hastily made for the refreshment room, where Lord Atwater brought them to a confused halt. Surprised by their sudden entrance, the earl hastily returned a fourth lobster patty to the platter. The gout had not dissuaded him from his usual habits of eating.

"Come in," the earl boomed. "Plenty of food for everyone. Might as well eat it up before they do." He jerked his head towards the billiard room. "Had more than enough of billiards, though I must say that I never enjoyed an evening more. What say you?"

"Er...yes..." The blue-eyed gentleman took a plate.

"Sent down from the University because of a scrape, I'll go bail?"

"That's right."

"Which one?"

"Cambridge," he replied at the same time that his companion came out with "Oxford."

The earl frowned. "Well, which is it?"

"Both, actually...he is at Cambridge and I at Oxford."

"Hmmph." The earl chewed on a lobster patty. "I'm all for Oxford myself," he said. "Spent my years there. Had a devilishly difficult time in Latin. Dragon of a professor. What was his name? Dickers. Is he still there?"

"Er, yes..."

"Really? Would be getting near on ninety."

"Er, the one I have now had a father who was himself a professor of Latin... that must be the one you had, sir."

"Possible. Except that I don't believe Dickers was married. Hated women. Wouldn't have anything to do with them."

"I believe he changed his attitude later in life."

The earl humphed and peered more inquisitively at the pair. But just then the match in the blue room concluded, and a steady stream of gentlemen began to parade through the doorway.

"Grab the lobster patties while you can!" the earl advised.

The college lads carried their laden plates out of the refreshment room and into the safety of an empty anteroom, where they soon fell laughing onto the crocodile-legged couch.

"Oh, Viv, I thought I would perish when Reed sauntered up to us," Rory exclaimed, emerging from her sister's embrace.

"So did I!" Viv averred, wiping her streaming eyes. "But not as much as when your grandfather began to quiz me about that Latin professor he once had at Oxford."

"Yes, and I thought it ever so clever of you to say that it was his son who was teaching you. I shouldn't have been able to think of something like that! Do you think anyone suspects?"

"Heavens, no!" Vivian exclaimed. She glanced into the pier-glass on the wall. With her dark hair pinned under a jet-black wig, her neckcloth imperfectly tied about her throat and that hideous olive-green coat, she looked like the furthest thing from a respectable young lady.

"I would have thought that Grandfather might recognize his old coats and shirts," Rory said, sampling a chicken leg.

"Oh, good gracious, no. These coats are far too old," Vivian reminded her. They had unearthed the clothing from a trunk in the attic two days before. Vivian had plied a needle like an expert, so without difficulty she had altered the garments to fit.

Their hair had been a trickier problem. Rory insisted that they should cut each other's curls, but Vivian fought shy of sacrificing her lustrous locks for one night's sport. She was not interested in attending every Wednesday soirée, just this one, to see for herself how the scheme had gone off. From the same trunk that held the earl's coats had come Lady Edwina's wigs, which they were able to trim enough to suit their purposes.

However, no amount of expertise with scissors or needle could camouflage a badly tied cravat. There had been no way of learning the rudiments of so masculine a skill in so short a time. Fortunately, in the Atwater library Vivian found a book on male fashion and was able to knot a rudimentary type of neckcloth such as those favoured by University youth.

She sat back now on the couch, reviewing the evening's events. She had thought it would be difficult to gain entry to Reed's establishment, so she and Rory had waited until a crowd of gentlemen boisterously demanded entrance in order to view the match and had slipped in with them.

Now, if they could only slip out without attracting notice, their night would be a success. And tomorrow she could turn Reed a deaf ear when he came calling with news of what had transpired at his billiard match.

Her lips curved in a secretive smile as she imagined the scene: Reed, tall and lanky, dressed to perfection as always, giving her his offhand assurance that the whole matter had gone prodigiously well, and her own equally offhand lack of interest. She could not decide whether to tell him of their hoax. Probably not. She knew his sense of propriety was very strict.

"As soon as we have eaten we shall have to be off," Vivian said to Rory now.

Her sister balked. "Why must we go so soon? I've barely consumed any of the tarts."

"While the gentlemen were absorbed in their billiards no one paid us a jot of attention. But now that the game is finished they might notice us, which will mean more attempts to draw us into conversation. I for one can do without more questions for this evening."

"In that case," Rory said, "I'd better eat, as I am famished."

She was also thirsty, and neither of them had had the foresight to bring anything to drink into the anteroom.

"I'll get something...." Rory volunteered, having finished her food first.

"None of the Madeira or claret," Vivian warned.

"Why not?"

"How would we explain your foxed state to Lady Edwina tomorrow? She'd be bound to think that you were ill and begin to quack you."

"They won't have lemonade or ratafia here," Rory pointed out.

"Then a glass of champagne." Shared between the two of them, the champagne would not do much harm.

After Rory left on this errand, Vivian reapplied herself to the plate in front of her. She was very hungry. She had just taken a bite of chicken when the door to the anteroom opened. She nearly choked when she looked up and recognized Lord Trawley.

"How now." Trawley frowned. "I had no idea this room was occupied."

Vivian chewed and swallowed the chicken, thinking furiously. Was her disguise good enough to pass close scrutiny by Trawley?

"Tired of the noise and confusion," she said, remembering to keep her voice as low as possible. Something that was more difficult than she had first thought.

"So am I. What's your name?" the viscount asked, sitting down and clapping her on the shoulder so strongly that she felt her breath taken away.

"Vi-Vincent Cartwith."

"Cartwith? Where's your family from?"

"The south."

"Kent?"

"No, I mean yes." It was no use. She was not good at dissembling and never had been. Besides, Trawley was a friend who would probably enjoy the hoax.

With one hand Vivian yanked off her wig, causing her reddish-brown curls to cascade to her shoulders.

"Miss Spalding!" Trawley turned nearly as rigid as his collar points. "What are you doing here?"

"Enjoying the billiard matches," she replied.

"Does Reed know you have been under his roof? He won't be pleased."

"No, and pray don't tell him. He'll call it hoydenish of me."

"It is most unusual for a female to be alone amidst so many gentlemen."

"But I'm not alone. Rory is with me."

The viscount looked thunderstruck. "Rory! By Jove, Miss Spalding. If you don't worry about your reputation, you should spare some thought for your sister's. I should tell Reed. You ought not to be here. You should be—"

"Back at Hill Street, twiddling my thumbs," she finished with a flare of temper. "Much fun that would be."

"Fun will be the ruin of you, Miss Spalding. Just where is Miss Rory?"

"She went to fetch us something to drink."

"Once Rory has returned, I shall escort the two of you back to Hill Street."

"Agreed. And I wish you would not poker up so. I only let you in on our secret because I thought you would enjoy it. Don't you think our disguises very clever?"

A reluctant smile creased his face.

"By disguise do you mean that antiquated wig, and that badly cut coat, and that horror of a neckcloth?"

"I thought my neckcloth creditable enough for an Oxford lad," she retorted.

"You do the entire line of lads from Oxford a disservice by that cravat. Come over to this mirror," he commanded. "I shall show you how to tie it properly."

Once there, he untied his own cravat and bade her follow his instructions, but these were so complicated that it gave her the headache.

"No, it is no use!" she groaned. "And it is to no purpose. I don't intend to take up this disguise ever again."

"I shall do it for you, but you must pay attention," he said, folding it over once, twice and thrice. But her attempts to follow his lead only brought on an attack of the giggles.

"You are not paying attention."

"I am," she protested.

So absorbed were they in their neckcloths that they failed to hear the door behind them open.

"Here now! Miss Spalding! What the devil are you doing here? And who's that with you? Trawley?"

Lord Atwater's normally ruddy complexion turned apoplectic as he viewed his American guest in a state of *déshabillé*.

"Oh heavens, my lord," Vivian exclaimed. "You have found us out. Pray, don't be too harsh on me. I would come, even though the gentlemen ordered me not to."

To her surprise Atwater swept past her without another word, to fix a baleful stare on the viscount.

"Trawley, you will explain how my granddaughter's sister comes to be in your company with her clothing askew and your own in equal disarray."

Vivian's brows shot up as she realized instantly the false impression she and Trawley had given the earl.

"Lord Atwater, you are mistaken. Our clothing is askew because Trawley was teaching me—"

"Silence!" the earl thundered, lifting a hand. "I know just the sort of lessons he undertakes for young ladies. Trawley, I am waiting for an explanation."

"I bid you wait no longer, my lord," Trawley drawled, "for I'm sure you will wish us happy when I tell you that Miss Spalding and I are going to be married!"

"Going to be *what?*" Vivian exclaimed, turning an incredulous countenance to the gentleman next to her.

"Married," Trawley replied, fortifying himself with a pinch of snuff.

"Marriage!" Lord Atwater beetled his brow. "Something havy-cavy's going on here."

"Nothing havy-cavy, my lord. I do hope you approve of the match," Trawley said, taking Vivian's hand firmly in his.

"He may approve," Vivian interjected, "but I don't need—"

"To have his approval, yes, I know, my dear," Trawley said, directing a quelling look her way. "You are an American, and they are very attached to notions of equality."

"But I still don't understand what you are doing here, dressed like that, engaged to be married or not," the earl said fretfully.

Vivian hesitated, not wishing to reveal Rory's part in the scheme to her grandfather.

"It was a hoax concocted for my amusement, sir," Trawley replied.

"Humph," the earl snorted. "Seems to me that you'd better marry her straight off and have enough of such hoaxes."

He left the room, affording Vivian her first opportunity to demand that the viscount explain his presumptuous words.

"Have you gone mad? The very idea of marriage! You must be out of your head."

"I wish I were," he said, looking far from loverlike himself. "Dear Miss Spalding, you don't realize that your little prank has cost you dearly. And cost me, as well."

"I could have explained to Rory's grandfather. You shouldn't have told him that you wished to marry me. You don't, do you?" she asked uncertainly.

"No! But that won't prevent me from doing the deed at the proper time."

"I'll explain."

"Any explanations will only sully your reputation. I am considered a loose screw in our Society. If only you had gone for the champagne instead of Rory."

Her eyes narrowed as she wondered what to make of this remark.

"I'm sure another solution will arise."

"There is none," Trawley said glumly. "I may have been accused of ruining a lady's reputation before, but never a truly honourable one like you. I have my faults, but that much of a blackguard I am not."

Vivian shook her head, as though to clear it of cobwebs. "But I can't marry you."

"Should we not marry and should the story become known, you would be ostracized."

"Fiddle. I've been ostracized before."

"Not like this," he warned. "You'd not have a shred of reputation left. Any female found alone in my company is advised to marry quickly."

She inhaled a breath, thinking hard. There had to be some way out of this muddle.

"I have no objection to your telling people we are going to be married in order to make my days in London more comfortable. But the marriage itself won't be necessary. I will return to America," she explained. "You do see that that is the perfect answer. My reputation will be considered quite safe there. And you will be able to go on as you are."

He paused. "And Rory? Would she go with you?"

"That would be up to her," she said. "And where is she, I wonder? She has been gone an inordinate amount of time just to fetch some champagne."

She replaced her wig and, with Trawley's assistance, tied her cravat once more. Then the two of them left the anteroom and discovered Rory, drinking champagne and listening to the tales of a cock-fight some of the younger sprigs were relating.

In answer to the summons in Vivian's eye, Rory drew apart from her new friends and sauntered over.

"I was just bringing you the champagne, Viv."

"And drinking more than one yourself. Come. Trawley knows the truth about us and is seeing us home."

"Why must we go so soon?" Rory asked, turning a pleading face towards the viscount. "I've just been listening to the most rivetting tale of a cock-fight."

The viscount shuddered. "Next, it will be bear-baiting."

"There's Reed," Vivian interjected. "Thank heaven, he is not looking our way. We can sneak out the door."

Quickly the three of them hurried out. Vivian did not feel truly safe until they were in Trawley's carriage.

"Why do we have to go?" Rory asked, looking mulish.

"Your grandfather recognized me."

"Grandfather!" Rory turned white. "Did he come back to question you more about Oxford?"

Vivian thrust her hands into the pockets of the olive coat.

"He came into the anteroom where Trawley was teaching me the rudiments of tying a cravat and mistook the matter."

"Mistook it how?"

Trawley and Vivian exchanged glances.

"He thought I was making love to your sister," he said bluntly.

"What? To Vivian?" Rory burst into giggles. "I should have liked to have seen his face!"

"It is not that impossible an occurrence," she said sternly. The colour was high in her cheeks and she felt the urge to box her sister's ears.

"I duly explained to your grandfather that Miss Spalding and I were going to be married," Trawley said, watching Rory under lazy lids.

The laughter faded from Rory's blue eyes.

"Married? But you are jesting, surely."

Trawley shook his head. "I never jest about marriage."

"The wedding will not come to pass," Vivian said. "I shall return to America."

"Oh, but you can't. Not yet, when things are going so well for us."

Vivian's eyebrows lifted. She and Rory had been ostracized from Society and now she was spoken for in matrimony by a rakish viscount. If this was how things went well...

Once they arrived back at Hill Street another vexing problem arose. How would they make their way upstairs? Lady Edwina's window was still lit up and they could not chance her encountering them in gentlemen's attire.

"We'll have to climb up that chestnut tree," Vivian said, pointing to the branches reaching towards their second-storey bedchamber.

"I'll hold your coats," Trawley said and took them while the two ladies scaled the tree.

Fortunately, girlhoods spent exploring the open country around Philadelphia had made both Spaldings experts at climbing trees and they soon reached their window. It was wedged shut, but together they were able to open it and squeeze through.

Trawley watched them wave, then saw them disappear from the window. Deep in thought, he returned to his carriage, still carrying their coats.

"VIVIAN, WHY DON'T YOU want to marry Trawley?" Rory asked as she began to undress. "Is it because everyone says he is a loose screw?"

"Rory!" her sister replied, shocked that Rory should have heard such rumours. "That's not it at all. He merely offered for me out of duty. I'm not marrying anyone. I'll just go back to America."

"Mama will pinch and scold you until there is no bearing it."

"I shall bear it," Vivian said with a sigh. She took off her wig and began to draw a silver-handled brush through her dark hair. "I must."

"I wish you would stay here in England with me."

Vivian undressed and changed into a nightgown, shoving the wigs, Hussar boots, pants and frilled shirts into the corner of the wardrobe. She would return them to the attic tomorrow.

Her sister blew out the candle and got into bed. "Is there no Englishman whom you could love and marry and stay in England with?" she asked sleepily.

"No one comes to mind."

Rory yawned. "What about Reed?"

"Reed is practically betrothed to Miss Long."

"Yes, but you know they are quarrelling. You could very easily cut her out."

Vivian felt an unwarranted thrill of pleasure at that idea. But it was too stupid. Miss Long was beautiful and fashionable.

"Even if he does quarrel with Miss Long, her successor must be cut from the same fashionable cloth. Do go to sleep. The very idea is silly."

"No more silly than your marrying Trawley."

"I am not marrying him," Vivian said, and went to bed where she lay awake, wondering just how a veritable American nobody *could* cut out an aristocratic beauty like Astrid Long.

CHAPTER NINE

As THE ONE O'CLOCK HOUR sounded on the grandfather clock in his hallway, Reed smothered a yawn. His supply of Madeira and claret had given out, but still one last guest lingered to sample the remainder of the French delicacies.

"Compliments to your chef, Lucian," Lord Atwater said, smacking his lips.

"Thank you, Charles. I trust you are fully recovered from the gout?"

The earl winced. "No, don't mention the gout. A man has a right to enjoy himself, doesn't he?"

"So he does. You had an enjoyable evening, then?"

"Aye, though it had all the makings of a bumblebroth for a moment there."

"Are you referring to the match between Edgewater and Harvey, when Harvey coughed just as Edgewater was hunched over his cue?"

"No, not that. I was talking about Trawley and Miss Spalding."

"Trawley and who?" Reed asked incredulously.

The earl instantly regretted his slip of the tongue. It would do no good to reveal to Reed that Vivian had been under his roof. Trawley had offered for her and that was the main thing.

"By Jove, look at the time. I must go." He thrust his plate at Reed.

"But what about Trawley and Miss Spalding?" Reed asked, following him towards the door, determined to learn more.

"He's made her an offer, and she's accepted," the earl said finally.

"An offer? Of marriage?" Reed's outraged look spoke volumes.

"Certainly of marriage," the earl said, exasperated. "Asked my permission. I haven't time to give you the details. You'd best ask him."

"You may rest assured I shall do so immediately," Reed promised.

He closed the door after the earl and stood for a moment, leaning against the solid oak, frowning in thought. He'd lost track of Trawley and had assumed the viscount had desired an early night. But to offer for Vivian Spalding! He must be all about in his head.

Charles must be mistaken. George had resisted all attempts to force him to marry any respectable female in the past. Why would he then offer for Miss Spalding? Could his offer of marriage to her really be heartfelt?

Without realizing what he was doing, Reed found himself in his carriage bound for Trawley's quarters. His mind dwelt momentarily on Fanchon's bills, which had been directed to the viscount for payment. The settlement of a wager. Now the offer of marriage.

And why should it unsettle him so?

A few minutes later Reed faced Trawley's butler.

"I know it's devilishly late, Belt, but I need to have a word with your employer? Is he in?"

"Yes, Mr. Reed. His lordship is in, but he specifically asked not to be disturbed."

"Don't worry. I'll tell him you had nothing to do with my visit," Reed said, taking the stairs two at a time. He came to Trawley's dressingroom and opened without knocking. The room was lit, but there was no sign of George. Had he retired to bed already? As he prepared to close the door Reed's eyes spotted two coats lying in a crumpled heap in a corner. He picked them up and frowned. Not the kind of coat that Trawley favoured. They were much smaller and old-fashioned. That olive colour... His puzzlement changed into shock when he realized just where he had seen the coats before. On the backs of the two University lads.

Sits the wind in that quarter? he wondered. And why had he never noticed his friend's inclination in that direction before? Quickly, wanting to be far away before he caught Trawley *in flagrante delicto* with his young men, Reed spun on his heel and left the sittingroom. At the bottom of the stairs Belt waited with a lit taper.

"Was his lordship very angry, sir?" Belt enquired.

No wonder George had given his servant strict instructions not to be disturbed.

"No, I didn't get a chance to see him," Reed replied. "I changed my mind. I didn't want him to get on his high ropes about my barging in. I'll see him tomorrow at the club. Meanwhile, there is no necessity to tell him I came calling."

"Very good, Mr. Reed."

"OH, VIVIAN, MY HEAD IS splitting!" Rory moaned the next morning as she tossed and turned on the pillow. The merest motion of the coverlet being pulled down occasioned the most painful throbbing, as though her head were being sawed in two.

Her sister was surprisingly unfeeling.

"You deserve the headache for drinking all that champagne," Vivian said, ruthlessly pulling open the curtains.

"But I didn't know this would be the result," Rory protested, holding one hand up to her head. She attempted to sit up, but then fell back in bed.

"You will be fine by this afternoon," Vivian assured her. "I once saw Papa totally foxed, but he was put to rights by day's end."

"Vivian, if you love me I pray you lower your voice. You are shouting so," Rory whispered.

Vivian laughed and, taking pity on her sister, soaked a handkerchief in lemon water and laid it on her temples. She would need to invent a tale about why Rory had taken to her bed, one that would forestall Lady Edwina and her arsenal of potions.

"What you need is rest. I shall draw the curtains for you."

"Remind me never to drink champagne again," Rory said plaintively as Vivian left the room.

"WHERE IS RORY?" LADY Edwina asked as she presided over the coffee urn in the breakfast parlour.

"She felt unwell so I left her resting abovestairs," Vivian said.

Lady Edwina rose, prepared to do battle with the grippe or even scarlet fever.

"I do think she ought to be allowed to rest. It might be something she ate."

"Something she ate? Do you mean the food was tainted?"

"Not exactly. I just think that perhaps she ate too much and is feeling unwell."

"I thought that fish the other day looked strange, even though François camouflaged it in that sorrel sauce. I shall go directly and tell him so!"

The ensuing battle that erupted in the kitchens as Lady Edwina interrogated the toplofty chef employed by her brother could be heard by all in the household, with the end result that the chef departed, carrying only his hat and his favourite saucepan.

Guilt-stricken at what had taken place because of her Banbury Tale, Vivian attempted to dissuade the chef from departing.

"It is not the first time this has happened, Mademoiselle," François said. *"Adieu."*

The news of François's abrupt departure brought the earl from his bedchamber. But Lady Edwina stood firm.

"Now you won't be gorging yourself on those cakes and pastries," she reminded her brother, who was devilishly fond of those cakes and pastries. The earl wondered gloomily if he could take all his meals at White's until François could be coaxed into returning.

"I should advise you to eat a hearty breakfast," the earl said to Vivian in the breakfast parlour. "Won't know when there will be anything edible in the house again. I overheard Edwina say that she is meaning to try out some new recipes which are supposed to restore one to the peak of health. Being restored to the peak of health," he divulged as he helped himself to a portion of ham, "usually means swallowing some vile concoction."

"François will return, won't he?"

"Oh, yes. It stands to reason. Just won't know when, that's all. Once he stayed away for two weeks. I was nearly skin and bone by then," he said, patting his ample stomach absent-mindedly. "But enough of François; I would be failing in my duty as your host if I did not tell you that your behaviour last night was not that of a respectable young lady."

"I'm sorry, my lord."

"Humph. Sorry is as sorry does. I might have expected as much from Rory, young as she is and prone to pranks, but you are older and ought to know better." He speared some ham and chewed thickly. "You should be thanking your stars that Trawley offered for you. Can't begin to count the number of females he's rumoured to have ruined." He put down his fork, realizing that he was discussing a delicate matter with a young lady. "Beg pardon. I shouldn't say that about him now that he's going to be your husband. And I must own I was relieved that he did offer for you. Thought he wouldn't do the proper thing. A pretty business that would be!"

"I know. I wouldn't have a shred of reputation left to me."

"You?" The earl snorted. "I wasn't talking about you. I was talking about me. I'd be obliged to call Trawley out, and at my age I don't relish a duel at dawn."

Such an idiotish idea had never occurred to Vivian.

"Why would you duel with Trawley?" she asked, astonished.

"You're my granddaughter's sister, my responsibility in England. Can't have anyone ruining you and not paying for it. So his offer and your marriage saves me from having to meet him at Paddington Green."

"I see."

Vivian finished her breakfast and went up to check on Rory, who was sleeping fitfully. She had half expected Reed to call this morning to relate what had happened at the tournament, so she was not surprised to find the butler seeking her out a half hour later. But when she went into the blue drawingroom she found not Reed but Miss Fortescue, a petite blonde, and Miss Peabody, a comely redhead.

She had been introduced to both young ladies earlier in the week and thought them agreeable enough, though under the thumbs of their mothers. Thankfully, there was no sign of their mothers this morning.

"Good morning, Miss Peabody, Miss Fortescue."

"Good morning, Miss Spalding," Miss Peabody said, her hands fluttering weakly to her chest. "I hope you don't mind our just descending on you this way."

"Not in the least. It has been several days since I've had a caller."

"Yes, we know," Miss Fortescue said, then coloured.

"Miss Spalding, we didn't mean to turn you a cold shoulder the other day on the street, but our mothers said if we did not we would suffer the consequences from the Patronesses," Miss Peabody said in a rush.

"And yet you find your courage now to risk their wrath?"

Miss Peabody blushed. "Yes. Last evening was so difficult." She glanced over at Miss Fortescue and then burst into tears.

Rather alarmed at this transformation of her guest into a watering-pot, Vivian was at a loss over what to do. Miss Fortescue, however, thrust a hartshorn under her friend's nose.

"Now, Emily, don't be a goosecap. Miss Spalding will help you. Won't you, Miss Spalding?"

"If I can. What kind of help do you desire?"

Miss Peabody emerged from her handkerchief. "You don't understand. Papa is going to make me marry odious Lord Steiker and I don't want to!"

"I'm very sorry—"

"Miss Spalding, can you tell us why Lord Ludwin stayed away from Almack's last night?"

"Ludwin?"

"Papa had been expecting that Ludwin would come up to scratch, as they say, and offer for me soon. Last night at Almack's, we were so hoping. But he did not appear. He has been dangling after me, along with several other gentlemen. Papa had told me that if Ludwin offered he would accept the offer on my behalf, which is the dearest wish of my heart. He is so dashing and handsome. But if he doesn't come to Almack's next week and let Papa know that he's serious about me, Papa will marry me off to Lord Steiker, who is sixty and reeks of wine."

"He has been married twice before. Each time his wife died. They say that he murdered them!" Miss Fortescue revealed with ghoulish enthusiasm. "You must see that her situation is desperate."

All Vivian saw was that Miss Fortescue had a flair for the dramatic. Murdered wives, indeed.

"And you are destined to marry someone else, too?" Vivian enquired of Miss Fortescue.

"No, I am here to bear Emily company." Her cheeks turned pink. "But I did wonder if perhaps Lord Moreton would be attending Almack's next week."

Vivian recalled that Moreton had bested Mr. Henderson in his billiard match, so that in all likelihood he would be at Reed's next week.

"I would not count on Moreton attending Almack's," she said.

Miss Fortescue's eyes clouded with obvious disappointment.

"Almack's is nothing without the gentlemen," Miss Peabody moaned into her handkerchief. "And my new ball gown was ever so expensive. When will it end? When will the gentlemen return?"

"As soon as the Patronesses apologize to Mr. Reed and Lord Trawley."

Miss Peabody and Miss Fortescue exchanged stricken looks. "I am doomed," Miss Peabody said. "The Patronesses will never apologize."

"If they want their gentlemen back, they shall have to," Vivian said. Reed's plan was going off without a hitch. And yet her heart was touched by Miss Peabody's situation.

"Perhaps you will see Ludwin during the week at another soirée," she said, encouraging her guest to look on the brighter side of things.

"I hope so."

"I've never seen Almack's so deserted," Miss Fortescue said as they took their leave. "I was even obliged to stand up with that odious Mr. Clive."

AT WHITE'S, MEANWHILE, the odious Mr. Clive was regaling the other gentlemen with stories of his triumphs with the Season's new Beauties. His words were greeted with hoots of disbelief.

"They did dance with me!" he insisted stoutly, rather incensed that no one believed him. "Go and ask them."

"I shouldn't embarrass any female by asking any such thing," one wag replied. "Admit to dancing with you! Any respectable female would deny it."

There was a roar of agreement and laughter. Beet-red, Mr. Clive pushed his way through the crowd of gentlemen.

"Will you be ready for next Wednesday?" someone asked Ludwin.

"I shall be practising diligently all week," the marquis replied.

"Good. I have a hundred pounds on you."

Reed was seated in the readingroom and frowned as he heard the voices in the hallway, taking or offering wagers on the billiard match. His views on gaming were well known, but he could not prevent anyone from wagering on the outcome of the tournament. Had he been a betting man, he would have put his money on Moreton, who had as soft a touch as anyone with a cue stick.

"So here you are, Lucian." Viscount Trawley dropped a friendly hand on Reed's shoulder. "Sorry I dashed off last night without saying a proper adieu."

"It wasn't important," Reed said, wondering at the easy charade Trawley had adopted during the years. His reputation as a seducer of young ladies was the perfect camouflage for his real interest in young men like the University pair.

"By all rights we gave the Patronesses a jolt," Trawley went on. "If Clive played the role of the leading gentleman, the poor ladies of Almack's have had an unpleasant time of it."

"How long have you been so concerned with the young ladies of Almack's?" Reed asked ironically.

His friend gave a rueful laugh. "I suppose you're right. They don't exactly approve of me, do they?"

"You must admit, George, sometimes your behaviour comes close to deliberately courting disapproval."

The viscount was taken aback. Was it his imagination, or was his friend colder than usual to him? He put it down to the fuss and botheration of the tournament the night before.

He picked up a journal and then immediately put it down. "I don't know why I bother to read this. I shall be asleep in a moment." He yawned. "I had very little sleep last night."

Reed's lip curled. He wasn't interested in Trawley's escapade. He still found it hard to believe. Just as he found it hard to believe that the viscount would offer for Miss Spalding.

"I suppose we shall be reading something of interest in the *Gazette* soon enough concerning you," he said now.

Trawley looked puzzled.

"Your announcement," Reed said. "I spoke with the earl last night. He seemed to think that you and Miss Spalding were to be married. My felicitations. I was quite bowled over."

"I suppose you are wondering how it all came about," Trawley said, not wanting to lie to his friend.

"You fell top over tail in love with her, I daresay," Reed said, watching him carefully. "Her coppery hair, the curve of her lips when she smiles, the lithe but curvaceous figure."

"Good God, no!" Trawley ejaculated. "That's not to say that she's not pretty, because she is. If one's tastes run in that direction."

Reed flung down his newspaper.

"Spare me any further words, George. I know the truth about the University pair you were with last night."

"Do you, by Jove?" Trawley asked quickly. He had expected his friend to be angry at the hoydenish trick the Spaldings had played, but the emotion on Reed's face was not anger, but disgust.

"I'm glad you know. It isn't easy to deceive you, Reed. But it isn't as bad as you think it," he said quickly.

"In some circles I'm sure it is considered quite respectable," Reed said derisively. "How can you take advantage of Miss Spalding's ignorance about such matters?"

The viscount looked totally bewildered. "Advantage? Ignorance? She found herself in the suds and I did her a favour."

"And we both know why, don't we?" Reed said grimly, stalking out of the door, leaving the viscount with the inevitable belief that poor Lucian was even more strait-laced than one had suspected.

TWIRLING HIS malacca cane, Reed approached Lord Atwater's Town residence. He stood a moment, staring at the brass knocker, debating whether to poke his nose into something that had nothing to do with him. Of late he had found himself embroiled in other people's affairs.

No, not other people's affairs. Just one person: Miss Spalding's affairs. He scowled. Odious and disagreeable though it would be, he would have to persuade Miss Spalding to end her engagement to Trawley.

He sounded the knocker and was duly escorted into the blue drawingroom where Vivian found him some minutes later.

"Oh, Mr. Reed. How kind of you to call," she said, offering her hand. She had intended to be perfectly indifferent to his story about the billiard match, but the sight of him made her feel unexpectedly breathless and her hand tingled as his larger one engulfed it.

"Would you like a sherry?"

"No, thank you," he said, feeling a reluctance to let her hand leave his.

"Have you come to tell me about last night's event?" she asked as she seated herself on the satinwood sofa.

"Last night's event?" he repeated.

Her dark eyes widened. "The billiard match, sir."

He had forgot all about the billiard tournament. "Well yes, of course," he said. "It went tolerably well."

"Just tolerably well, sir?" Vivian asked. What a good thing she had sneaked into his residence! If this was the way he summed up last night's event...

"For the victors," Reed said, finding his thoughts drawn more to the tiny dimple in her chin than to the billiard match held last night. "And of course the victors advance into next week's round."

His mention of the next week's round brought Miss Peabody to Vivian's mind.

"Is it necessary for Lord Ludwin to play in the tournament next week?" she asked.

He frowned.

"I don't think it's a question of necessity, Miss Spalding. Nigel won his place in the tournament. He's in high gig and vowing to practise daily until next Wednesday."

"Oh, dear. Then I don't suppose you know if he is going to offer for Miss Peabody any time soon, do you?"

A more addled question he had never heard before. "What has Miss Peabody to do with anything?" he declared.

Vivian decided to be frank. "She visited this morning, quite agitated. It seems she is nursing a tendre for Ludwin. I hadn't realized the consequences of the plot we were hatching."

"Absence makes the heart grow fonder. If the chit waits patiently she'll land him."

"But she doesn't have much time. Her father is set to betroth her to Lord Steiker."

"Steiker?" Reed recoiled.

"You know the gentleman."

"Yes."

"Is he as bad as they say?"

"I don't know. He is very rich. Very fat, too. But I'm sure that Mr. Peabody would rather have Ludwin."

"Yes, but when will he offer for her?"

"Well, I don't know!" Reed expostulated. "I don't go about asking such things of gentlemen. He has his mind on the billiard match right now."

"You must remind him about Miss Peabody and her charms and sweet nature. You'd best tell him, too, that her father will not wait to betroth her to a gentleman. Under the circumstances he might give up the billiard tournament."

"What? After I've turned my household upside down to accommodate them? Can't tell him it's cancelled, because it's not. It's none of my affair, Ludwin's courtship, but—" he cleared his throat "—yours is."

She looked up, momentarily startled. "Mine, sir?"

"It's true, isn't it? Trawley's offered for you."

Her gaze fell, and she became aware of a disappointing lurch in her chest. "It's true," she agreed.

He leaned forward and cupped her chin, staring intently into her eyes.

"You must not accept his offer."

The impassioned look in his blue eyes brought a breathless hope to her breast. Was it possible that Reed might harbour some feeling for her? Or was that just wishing after stars? Was he about to make her a declaration himself?

"Why mustn't I, sir?" she asked softly.

"Because he... you... the two of you wouldn't suit," he said in strangled accents. How could he tell an innocent, unsuspecting female the truth about Trawley?

He let go of her chin and ran a finger between his neck and collar. This was much more difficult than he had imagined. "You have no idea the type of man he is. By reputation he is supposed to have ruined a dozen females." He glanced quickly at her, hoping that this hint would put her into enough of a fright to make her cry off.

But all she did was laugh.

"Good heavens, Mr. Reed. You make him out a veritable Bluebeard. Perceive me in a dreadful fright."

"Don't jest," he murmured. Try and do the chit a favour and see what results. There was no sense hinting about; he must say it directly. But how? "You don't know half the truth about Trawley."

"You are wrong. I know that his reputation is very bad, but I know he wouldn't ruin any female if he could help it."

"But he would take advantage of a female if he had better game afoot," Reed said, his lip curling.

Vivian stared. This personal attack on Trawley was not what she'd expect from Reed. Was it possible that Reed was jealous of Trawley?

"Mr. Reed, pray, why do you dislike the idea of a match between myself and Viscount Trawley?" she asked, determined to know what feelings he had for her, if any.

"Because you shouldn't marry him."

"Whom should I marry, pray?"

"Someone else."

"Who?" she asked, waiting for him to name himself.

Instead Reed rose and paced the length of the blue drawingroom.

"I don't know," he murmured.

Keenly disappointed, Vivian dropped her eyes from his handsome figure striding back and forth on the earl's prized Wilton.

"I'm not exactly in the habit of thinking about which gentleman you should marry," Reed went on, "except that I know you shouldn't marry George. You'd be saving yourself considerable grief if you would listen to me."

"If I had listened to you, I would be in the habit of taking my meals with the servants," she couldn't help reminding him.

"I thought you had forgiven my mistaking you for a governess? And it is to prevent you from making a more dire mistake that I am here today. Trawley's reputation as a seducer of women is a sham.''

"I am glad to hear it."

"Are you? It is a sham because he prefers to take young men to his bed!"

CHAPTER TEN

"How dare you say such a thing!" Vivian exclaimed.

"Believe me, I don't relish saying it," Reed countered, tugging at the folds of his snowy-white cravat. "But in perfect truth, Trawley is only offering for you to cover up his true nature."

Vivian stared at him. "You are unhinged," she said, not the least bit pleased by the assumption that only a man who preferred his own gender would offer her matrimony.

"I know it is a shock," Reed plunged ahead. "You could have bowled me over last night, but I have proof."

Vivian's brown eyes widened. Proof?

"Last night at my tournament there were two University lads," Reed said, sitting down once again next to her. "They were strange birds. Little more than youths."

"Really?" Vivian enquired, the light beginning to dawn.

"When I went over to see Trawley late last night to ask him about his offer for you, I discovered he was in his bedroom, asking not to be disturbed. The coats of the young men were on the floor of his sittingroom."

"And from this you deduce that his nature is turned in the direction of males?" she asked incredulously.

"It makes perfect sense," he said doggedly, "with all his protests about his reputation as a seducer of women. That's why he offered for you. It's the perfect camouflage."

A dangerous gleam glinted in Vivian's eyes as she plucked a thread from the hem of her blue day dress. "Those coats you saw, Mr. Reed. Would they be olive drab in colour, and badly out of mode, with six badly tarnished brass buttons?"

A black frown descended on his brow. "Yes, they would. But how do you know?"

"Because I was there, sir."

"With Trawley in his bedroom?" he asked, looking so stupefied that she burst into laughter.

"No, I was at your tournament. I was one of the University lads."

Reed was brought up short by this reply. "What!" he roared.

"Rory and I disguised ourselves and entered your establishment," she said, oblivious to his shock. "Lord Trawley saw through our disguise and escorted us home. We were obliged to climb the chestnut tree to make our way back to our bedchamber, so Trawley took our coats. That is how they came to be in his possession."

A muscle in Reed's jaw worked furiously. "You were at the billiard tournament? That is outrageous."

"No more outrageous than your thinking Trawley was—"

"I see your point," he said, cutting her off quickly. What a paperskull he'd been to have leapt to such an ill-considered conclusion about his friend. "Then your engagement is a true one?" he asked, feeling the seconds lengthening as she remained silent.

Vivian thought fleetingly of revealing the real circumstances behind Trawley's offer, but that would only lend credence to the previous belief that no gentleman would willingly offer for her—an opinion she found quite mortifying.

"Is it so impossible for a gentleman like him to offer for me?" she asked.

"Not impossible," Reed said. "But recalling all the ladies who would have marched him down the aisle at St. George's, I consider it most improbable."

"Improbable, is it?" Vivian stiffened, on the verge of hurling one of Lord Atwater's priceless Tang horses at the handsome but stupid man seated in the room with her.

"Don't get on your high ropes," he said, realizing that inadvertently he had once again offended her. Lightning bolts flashed in her dark eyes. Again he was reminded of claret, strong and dark enough to knock a man senseless. "Do you plan to marry George?" he asked, his voice sounding thick to his own ears.

"Can you give me any reason why I should not?" she asked quietly.

He stared at her, mesmerized by her eyes. He shook his head as though to clear it, a gesture she took as an answer to her query.

Briskly she rose from the chair to mask the disappointment she felt in her heart. "I must go abovestairs and look in on Rory," she said now. "She drank too much champagne at your event last night and is paying the penalty."

"Is she suffering the headache?"

"The headache is the least of it. Lady Edwina's cures are enough to make her vow never to touch a drop of champagne ever again."

"I shall take my leave then," he said, oddly troubled by the call, which had not gone as foreseen. "But before I go, there is just one favour I should like to ask of you, Miss Spalding."

A favour from her? After insulting her the way he had? "What is it?" she asked, curiosity getting the best of her.

"My nacky notion about George. If he ever got wind of that, there would be the devil to pay. His friendship matters to me. May I count on your silence regarding my unfortunate mistake?"

She liked Trawley and had no qualms about keeping her silence. Moreover, perhaps if she granted Reed this favour he would oblige her by helping Miss Peabody. After the last ten minutes Vivian was feeling keen sympathy for anyone in love.

"One favour easily granted, if you will grant one of yours," she said now.

"Which is?" he asked, cocking a mobile brow at her.

"Would you do all you can to encourage Lord Ludwin to remember Miss Peabody?"

"If it will save me from being run through on the tip of one of Trawley's swords, I will encourage Ludwin to remember every female he ever saw," Reed said promptly. "Why the sudden interest in Miss Peabody?"

Vivian was careful to keep her eyes on the floor as they crossed the black and white lozenges towards the door. "I felt so sorry for her. Being in love seems to be a most vexatious state of mind."

"So I've been told."

Involuntarily her gaze slid up his lanky frame to his face. "Have you never been in love, sir?"

"No. Should I have been?"

"I assumed that since you were practically betrothed to Miss Long—"

Reed was beginning to loathe the expression "practically betrothed," particularly when coupled with the name of Miss Long.

"My attachment to Miss Long is not based on romantic love."

"She must be a great heiress, then."

Reed drew himself up to his full height of six feet. "Not at all. The very idea."

"There is no need to take umbrage," she said. "It is certainly comforting to marry someone who is well dowried. I only hope that Trawley does not have much expectation from me there."

He frowned, not wanting to hear of Trawley's expectations of Vivian as his wife, but before either of them could say another word, Rory came bounding down the stairs.

"Viv, my headache is cured. I swallowed one of Aunt Edwina's smelly concoctions, but it did the thing and I'm well. Oh, I didn't know you were here, Mr. Reed."

"Good day, Miss Spalding," he said. "I came over to felicitate your sister on her coming marriage."

Rory laughed. "Do you mean to Lord Trawley? But that's just a hum—"

"Hummingbird?" Vivian said, quickly flinging the door open wide before Rory could make micefeet of everything. She stepped out into the London air. "It must have flown away, and since the wind is entirely too brisk, I must take my sister back inside. Good day to you, Mr. Reed."

"Good day," he said, rather surprised by these shifts which found him down the steps and the door to the earl's residence firmly closed. He clapped his beaver felt on his head and with a puzzled expression strolled down the street.

"Vivian, have you gone mad?" Rory declared when they were alone in the foyer. "Why did you do that? I didn't get a chance to talk to Reed about the tournament. Did you?"

"Yes, indeed. We talked about that and about Trawley's offer. He seemed to think that no man in his right mind would offer for me." She chewed on her lower lip. "I have half a notion to actually go ahead and marry Trawley."

"Vivian! You wouldn't, would you?" Rory asked, turning pale.

"I just might," Vivian said, looking grim and determined.

THE FIRST SALVO in the war against the Patronesses had been launched Wednesday evening, but it was not to be expected that those ladies would concede victory quickly. They appeared outwardly unchanged, nodding to their favourites in the street and snubbing those they had designated worthy of a snub. Still the tide of sentiment seemed to be rising inexorably against them. Rumours that the ton's Beauties would be boycotting Almack's next were rife, leading Lady Sefton to wonder if one ought to issue an edict against the Beauties, in which case they would soon be conversing with just themselves.

"Oh, do stop prattling like a ninnyhammer, Maria!" Countess Lieven exclaimed Friday morning in her drawing-room They were meeting to thrash out a solution to the problem.

Lady Sefton was usually the most placid of the Patronesses, but even she took umbrage at being stigmatized a ninny and retreated into a haughty silence at one end of the velvet settee.

It fell to Lady Jersey to play peacemaker, a role she handled with difficulty.

"Don't let's pull caps with each other," she said now. "We need a way out of this coil. I don't think I can hold my head up in public, and as for taking my usual drive in the Park today, that is out of the question."

"Your team will be glad to hear that," Countess Lieven mused aloud.

Lady Jersey glared, not pleased to be reminded about her lack of skill with the reins.

Princess Esterhazy plied a languid fan. "What we must do is to pretend nothing has gone wrong. The ton looks to us for leadership, and if we don't appear to think anything is amiss then they know it is not worth troubling themselves over."

Ordinarily this advice would have won some support, but Lady Jersey shook her head.

"They'll think we're blind. If we do nothing by the time next Wednesday comes we shan't have an Assembly worth the name. If the gentlemen leave, the ladies may soon follow."

"They wouldn't! Almack's is Almack's."

"Not without gentlemen."

"We would be meeting there all by ourselves," Lady Sefton said, her eyes filling with tears at the idea.

"Good gracious, what shall we do?"

By the end of an hour several suggestions had been proposed and rejected, including one by Mrs. Drummond Burrell that they cut the Season short. Over copious glasses of ratafia this was reviewed and disregarded, for to do so would inevitably lead to the rumour that Reed and Trawley had won.

"How did such a bumblebroth arise? I've always liked Reed. I can't say the same about Trawley, but Reed, I did like," Lady Jersey said.

"It came about because of your feathered hat!" Lady Sefton reminded her.

Lady Jersey was unwilling to bear the entire burden for the débâcle on her own shoulders.

"Seem to recall your niece, Astrid Long, was involved," she said, turning to Lady Sefton.

"Not a niece, a mere connexion."

"Whatever!"

"Don't mind telling you that she may be fashionable but butter wouldn't melt in her mouth," the countess said with a sniff of her aristocratic nose.

"But at least she attended the Assembly," Lady Sefton said darkly. "I have heard that Miss Fortescue won't."

"Why not?"

"Her father has always been against spending money on her and her wardrobe. He's done so only because it is necessary to dress her to attract some suitable gentleman. Now he says it is just a waste of time."

"*Au contraire.* Lord Moreton seemed close to putting his fate to the touch," the countess said.

Lady Jersey sipped her ratafia, wishing that the countess would serve something other than this vile drink. "That was before he touched a cue stick."

"It is this abominable billiard tournament. As long as Reed is holding it, the gentlemen will go there instead of to Almack's," Lady Sefton said.

"You are pudding-hearted to say such a thing!" Countess Lieven declared. "We shall hold Assembly at Almack's as usual. It shall be the most dazzling evening yet."

"Dreamer! It won't dazzle without gentlemen," Lady Jersey retorted.

The countess lifted the corners of her lips in a sibylline smile. "The gentlemen will be there," she prophesied.

"Would you care to make a bet?" Lady Jersey asked in a wagering mood.

The countess inclined her head. "Fifty pounds?"

"Done."

"But how will you get the gentlemen there when a billiard tournament is in progress at Reed's?" Maria Sefton pointed out the one impediment to this plan.

"Just wait and see," the countess said, continuing to look arch.

"What do you think she is up to?" Lady Sefton asked Lady Jersey as they drove away from the countess's residence. She hung on for dear life to the side of the carriage, since Lady Jersey was a poor hand at the reins.

"I don't know, but she is Russian, you must remember," Lady Jersey replied, frowning as she concentrated on the road ahead. "Perhaps she has something up her sleeve!"

WHAT THE COUNTESS HAD UP her sleeve was not at first apparent to anyone, including her fellow Patronesses, but by the week's end came enlightenment with the news that Tsar Alexander of Russia, travelling incognito, would be passing through Town.

"The Tsar!" Lady Edwina exclaimed to Vivian and Rory as they toured an exhibit of Mr. Turner's work at Somerset House. "My dears, that has stirred up the ton."

"What does Alexander look like?" Vivian asked, fingering the pearl buttons on her green walking dress. She had never seen a Russian before, let alone a tsar.

"Oh, he's ever so handsome and tall!" Lady Edwina said. "A prime favourite with the ladies. And the gentlemen say that he is pluck to the old backbone as well."

"You've seen him yourself?"

"No," she admitted. "But I did so want to see him. He is said to be a divine dancer. I shouldn't be at all surprised if he makes an appearance at Almack's."

"The Tsar at Almack's?" Vivian exclaimed. "Why would he go there?"

"Why shouldn't he?" Lady Edwina countered. "He knows the Countess Lieven. She is Russian, too. So I'm sure that nothing would please her more than to make an appearance there that night."

"How I wish I could see him!" Vivian exclaimed, after they had seen all the paintings.

"So do I," Rory added.

"Oh, my dears, I am sorry," Lady Edwina said guiltily. "I shouldn't have even spoken about Alexander since we won't be able to go to Almack's. The Patronesses haven't given you the vouchers, and without them—"

"You needn't explain, Aunt, we know," Rory said, patting her aunt's hand. "Besides, Alexander is probably a brutish oaf, not worth bothering about."

That Alexander was not a brutish oaf became apparent as the week wore on and more and more ladies hounded their modistes concerning their ball dresses for Wednesday evening. The gentlemen did not put themselves to as much concern with their apparel, but several sent Reed their regrets about attending the tournament.

"Nothing I'd enjoy more, but it's Alexander, you know!"

The defection of the gentlemen back to Almack's did not pass unnoticed by the Patronesses, who were seen once again in the Park in high fettle.

"How I detest the very sight of them," Reed complained to Trawley one morning. "Odious biddies."

"I do wonder how they managed to persuade Alexander to attend their Assembly."

"Only four billiard players are left." Reed jabbed his cane into the cobblestone street. "Blast and botheration."

"We can always post off for the country," Trawley told him. "I'm seeing to the renovations on my house."

Reed frowned, reminded in this offhand way that his friend would be shortly wedding Miss Spalding. Had he been wrong about the offer? Trawley was certainly giving the appearance of a man dangling after Miss Spalding. On the two occasions when Reed had stopped in at Hill Street, the viscount had been present.

"I think not," he said now in answer to Trawley's invitation. "I shall hold my tournament on Wednesday as planned."

"Then perhaps you will visit Trawle later in the month."

"Perhaps. Will Miss Spalding be one of your guests?"

"Very likely, but I shall have to ask her, shan't I?"

He put the question to Vivian the very next day during a morning drive.

"A visit to your country estate?" She twirled a fringed sunshade as she rode in his open carriage, enjoying the brisk May wind that brought colour to her cheeks. "That is kind of you, my lord."

"Bosh, least I could do to let you see more of England before you go."

"Go where?" she asked, confused.

"Go back to America," he said, taking his eyes off his pair of Welshbreds expertly turning a corner. "That is what you plan to do, isn't it?"

"Yes, of course," she said in a small voice. For some inexplicable reason she found Philadelphia less appealing than ever. "But we must pretend that we are going through with the marriage up to the moment I jilt you by stepping aboard my ship in Bristol. Otherwise Lord Atwater will suspect the hoax. He would then be obliged to call you out."

Trawley laughed. "You needn't worry," he assured her. "I shall be the devoted suitor. So devoted that I would wager anything I shall be pitied when I am jilted. That would be an interesting variation for me."

They rode on in a companionable silence, broken a few moments later with Vivian's query.

"Is Reed still holding his tournament on Wednesday?"

"Yes, and you are not to come to his residence," the viscount warned, "though I suspect that the University pair would be welcome since we are so thin of numbers."

Vivian, however, had decided that the University lads were more trouble than they were worth and did not plan to resurrect them.

"How many gentlemen have sent their regrets?"

"We are down to the four players and ourselves."

"Heavens. So few."

He nodded. "I told Lucian we ought to postpone the match, but he takes that as tantamount to surrendering to the Patronesses. It hardly seems worth the bother for anyone to appear. Ludwin is sure to win."

"Oh, is he still planning to attend?"

"Indeed, he is. Not even Alexander could woo him away from the cue."

Vivian wondered whether Reed had remembered to keep his promise about reminding the marquis about Miss Peabody.

In fact, much to his credit, Reed had remembered the promise he had made to Miss Spalding, and on meeting Ludwin at Weston's shop that same afternoon, attempted to speak to him on the matter of Miss Peabody.

"A charming lady, don't you think?" he asked, fingering the charcoal-grey coat the tailor was forming.

"Who? Emily? Yes, indeed. Sweet-voiced." The marquis held out his right arm so that Weston could measure a sleeve.

"Sweet-natured."

"Yes."

"I can't remember seeing a Beauty her equal."

"What about Miss Long?" Ludwin quizzed. "Thought you and she were—"

"No longer. We haven't spoken for at least a fortnight." For some reason this did not overset Reed. Against his will he thought of Vivian's audacious question about whether he loved Miss Long.

He had a question of his own for her: did *she* love Trawley?

Ludwin glanced over at Reed, who appeared to be in a brown study. If Reed had broken his tie to Astrid Long and was singing the praises of Miss Peabody, it could only mean one thing: he was dangling after Miss Peabody herself. The marquis held out his left arm for Weston, thinking it a great pity. He had been inclined to hope that Miss Peabody would look with favour on him, but if Reed favoured her for himself, he would step aside. It was the sporting thing to do.

Thinking of sport brought the tournament to mind and he cut short Reed's litany of praise for Miss Peabody.

"Donaldby tells me that he won't be competing tomorrow night."

"That's true. I vow the ranks of competition appear to be thinning rapidly. You needn't practise so vigilantly. I'm convinced that you will make the prize yours without any trouble at all."

Ludwin's usually cheerful face creased in a frown. "That's not very sporting, Reed. I want to win the championship properly, not because my opponent doesn't show up."

"I know," Reed inhaled a pinch of snuff. It was a new mixture and rather too dry for his tastes. "Alexander will be there on Wednesday evening."

"I don't see why everyone must gawk at a tsar."

Reed laughed. "Neither do I, for that matter, but Alexander is a prime attraction. No one would care a fig if

Prinny popped in at Almack's, but Alexander is a different kettle of fish."

JUST HOW DIFFERENT Alexander was could be known only to a few intimates in London, among them the Countess Lieven. Staring now at the recalcitrant figure in front of her, she brought her ivory-handled fan down smartly against his knuckles.

"Ow! Cousin, that hurts."

"And well it should, dear Klaus, if I ever hear you say another word about not attending Almack's on Wednesday."

The gentleman sucked on his bruised knuckles. "Why must I come as Cousin Alexander?"

"Because that's who they want," the countess replied. "There is no reason to be in a quake. Fortunately I have one of his uniforms, which he always wears. You are of the same height, and the resemblance is uncanny."

"But I thought he was supposed to be incognito. Why the uniform?"

"He was travelling to England incognito, but once at Almack's he will be seen in uniform—or rather *you* will be seen in uniform."

"But the minute I say a word, they'll know I'm not Alexander. My English is not as good as his," Klaus protested, the vacuous expression in his eyes more pronounced than ever.

"Then you must not say a word!" she reminded him with another rap on the knuckles. "You are to make an appearance at ten. You will bow to the ladies and kiss their hands. Speak Russian. No one here knows it very well."

"Good thing," he muttered.

"Be quiet and listen, dolt! You will make a point of dancing with me and then you will leave. Nothing could be simpler."

"If it's so simple, why don't you find someone else to do it," he whined.

"Because I am asking you," the countess said, her eyes narrowing into slits. "And need I remind you of the thousand pounds I loaned you when you were up the river tick?"

"Oh, very well, then," he replied and took the uniform away to try on.

CHAPTER ELEVEN

LONDON BUZZED of nothing but Tsar Alexander's impending visit.

"What a pity Lord Trawley took our coats away or we might be able to sneak into Almack's dressed as gentlemen!" Rory said to Vivian, as they sat in the music room, practising scales and wracking their brains to devise a scheme in which they might meet Alexander.

"Heavens, we wouldn't be allowed into Almack's, dressed like that!" Vivian said with a shudder.

"Then how are we to see the Tsar?" her sister demanded.

Vivian frowned at the music sheet in front of her, which in no way resembled the tune her fingers were playing on the keyboard.

"We won't, more's the pity. Do be sensible, Rory. We can't go as ourselves, and we can't go as gentlemen, so we shall be obliged to sit at home. And perhaps it might be disloyal of us if we *did* manage to make our way into Almack's."

"What do you mean 'disloyal?'" Rory asked immediately.

"Reed's tournament," Vivian explained. "It's goose to guineas that Almack's will be fuller of company than expected because of Alexander, and that means fewer gentlemen will be at Reed's."

"Oh. I hadn't thought of that. Will it look as though the Patronesses have won?"

"I fear so," Vivian said with a sad nod.

"Then I don't care a rush about sneaking into Almack's any more," her sister declared. "What we must do is sneak into the tournament again so that he has some other gentlemen at his party."

"Oh, Rory, you are impossible. If we did sneak into Reed's with so few men in attendance, how long do you think it would be before someone discovered the cheat? How very shocked they would be. And only think what damage to our reputations! Trawley can't marry two of us, you know."

Rory glanced up from the pianoforte. "I know," she said in a small voice.

Since neither of them was making much progress with their music, they turned to the more appealing pastime of cards. Vivian shuffled and dealt. She supposed that when she did make the inevitable trip back to America she would have to bring her cards with her, so she could amuse herself.

So absorbed was she in the game with Rory that they failed to hear Lady Edwina come in until she was standing right behind Vivian.

"What are you playing, my dears?"

"We started off with Patience," Rory explained. "But Vivian has been attempting to teach me the difference between long whist and short."

"A prodigious undertaking," her aunt said with a smile.

"I hope you are not shocked, ma'am," Vivian said. "Our father taught me the rudiments of handling a deck at an early age. Did you want us for some particular reason, ma'am?"

"Ah, yes, Charles is in his library asking for you, Vivian. He is preparing to write your father about your engagement to Trawley and thought he would speak to you first."

Her engagement to Trawley! Vivian had forgot that to the earl her engagement was a serious offer indeed. She flew down the Adam staircase, trailed by Lady Edwina, who offered her felicitations on the engagement.

"I must confess to some surprise. I saw not a hint of partiality in either of you before this."

"It was very sudden," Vivian agreed, one hand clutching the balustrade.

"Will you be having the wedding here in London or in the country?" Lady Edwina asked, unable to rein in her curiosity.

"I don't know."

"His mother will no doubt have some say in the nuptial arrangements."

His mother? She had been unaware that Trawley had a mother still living.

"She never paid any attention to the ladies he's supposed to have ruined, but I think she will extend herself to find out about a lady he intends to marry."

Unable to face any more questions from Lady Edwina, Vivian fled into the earl's library.

Lord Atwater waved her into the seat opposite his malachite desk and put down the quill he had been using.

"Come in, Vivian. I have been writing to your father. Trying to write, I should say." He pointed gloomily to the crushed pieces of paper littering the desk. "Can't seem to get the words out."

"I know the feeling, sir."

"Do you?" He brightened. "Never was much of a hand at writing compositions. And what do I say to a son-in-law? My daughter never writes to me anymore."

Vivian felt a pang of sympathy for the earl. Lady Pamela was his only child, and she was far away in Philadelphia. It must have been a lonely life for him after his wife died.

"You are good to be concerned, my lord," she said now. "But I shall write to Papa sometime soon."

"Of course I'm concerned. Since you've been here these few weeks, I've grown fond of you, Vivian. Almost as fond of you as I am of Rory."

"You and Lady Edwina have been kindness itself," Vivian said, much touched.

"Then help me with this dratted letter to your father," he commanded.

After half an hour a very decent composition had been penned, informing Mr. Thomas Spalding that his daughter, Vivian, had with the earl's permission engaged herself to the Viscount Trawley.

The earl blotted and sealed the letter. "That's over, I'm glad to say. Never did like writing letters overmuch. Getting them is another story, of course. Just got finished a letter from Montcalm. He is on the staff of the Viceroy to India. Says that they expected a visit from the Tsar, but he had to return to St. Petersburg. Something about a crisis at court. Probably some addled person plotting an overthrow."

"The tsar? Which tsar is that?"

The earl laughed. "You Americans! You know nothing about European geography. There's only one Tsar, my dear. Alexander."

"Really? When was the letter written, sir?"

"Three weeks ago."

"Do you think Alexander is in St. Petersburg now?"

"Probably. Montcalm said the roads were poor, but by now he is back in his homeland."

"But there must be some mistake. He can't be in Russia."

"Why not? Terribly fond of their homeland, these Russians, I knew a Cossack once..."

Vivian listened patiently to the tale of the homesick Cossack. "Nevertheless the Patronesses expect Alexander this week at Almack's."

"They do?" the earl asked. He had been confined to his room with another painful episode of gout and had not stirred outside his residence.

"It must be some other Alexander," he said now. "Montcalm is never wrong with his facts. If he says the Tsar was returning to Russia, that's where he is."

THE TALL, DARK-HAIRED MAN strolling down Bond Street turned as he heard his name called out. The inquisitive look on his handsome face turned to amazement as he recognized Miss Spalding.

"What are doing here?" he asked.

Vivian had caught sight of Reed ten minutes earlier when she, Lady Edwina and Rory were entering Madame Fanchon's shop. She left her sister behind with Lady Edwina and had hurried after Reed, wanting to tell him about Alexander. This was not as easy as she had thought. His much longer stride forced her to take two steps for every one of his and by the time she caught up to him at Bond Street she was out of breath.

"I must speak to you," she said, gasping a little.

With difficulty Reed forced his eyes away from the bodice of her Chinese-red walking dress, which rose and fell with each breath she drew.

"Miss Spalding, no doubt females in Philadelphia are accustomed to racketing about wherever they wish without a maid, but in London it is not the thing for a female to stroll down Bond Street without one, particularly in the afternoon." His ivory-handled walking stick jabbed at a loose cobble-stone.

Her brown eyes slanted quizzically up at him. "Why?"

With some difficulty he pulled his gaze from hers. There should be a law against ladies possessing eyes as bewitching as hers, he thought fretfully.

"Have you never heard the phrase the 'Bond Street beaux'?" he enquired now, speaking more frostily than necessary. *She was betrothed to Trawley*.

"If you mean that gentlemen may perhaps attempt to speak to me—"

"That's not all they will attempt to do," he said with a laugh. "Any female alone is fair game."

"But I'm not alone. Rory and Lady Edwina were with me. And now *you* are with me. No one need know about the ten minutes between then and now," she said with an impish grin.

He was about to return the grin but caught himself in time.

"If you do not care about your reputation, think of Trawley's. You are soon to be his wife. If George were here he would give you a thunderous scold."

To his surprise Vivian merely threw back her head and laughed. The sight of her long white throat and her head of coppery curls sparked an unmistakable longing in Reed. *She is Trawley's,* he reminded himself yet again, his grip tightening on his cane.

"What is so amusing?" he enquired.

"That Trawley should scold me about my reputation. His own is hardly without blemish. And I don't need to be scolded by him, when you are here to provide that necessary service," she pointed out. "Why is it that you delight in scolding me, sir?"

Because if he didn't scold her he'd probably kiss her senseless and that would land them in suds, Reed thought. He'd start with that white hollow of her throat and lead up to those ruby lips. And one kiss would lead inevitably to another and another. With difficulty he realized she had asked him yet another question.

"What did you say?" he asked thickly.

"I said that Trawley couldn't give me a better scold than you do. And I'm not even going to be your wife, am I?"

This innocent question triggered another most disconcerting pang in Reed's chest.

"Certainly not," he said, speaking more gruffly than before.

He became aware that their conversation had attracted the interest of passers-by and lowered his voice. "What is so important that you had to run from Bruton Street to New Bond Street to speak to me?"

She stared at him, almost forgetting how eager she'd been to share the news about the bogus Alexander with him.

"It's about Tsar Alexander," she said.

A nauseated look passed over Reed's face. "Oh, good Jupiter, don't mention him to me. I suppose you are utterly besotted by him and want to see him at Almack's like every other baconbrained chit in London."

"No, I do not," she retorted. "Unless, of course, it were the real Alexander."

Reed's blue eyes narrowed. "What do you mean, 'the real Alexander'?"

Quickly she related the news contained in Lord Montcalm's letter to the earl.

"Alexander called back to St. Petersburg?" Reed said, stroking his chin. "Are you certain?"

"You may ask the earl yourself. Of course, Lord Montcalm could be spinning a tale."

"No, his integrity is impeccable. But if Alexander was on his way to St. Petersburg three weeks ago, could he possibly make it over to London now?" Reed frowned. "No, there's too much land between the cities. The Patronesses are up to mischief. They haven't landed him for Wednesday evening. It's a hoax."

Vivian nodded, pleased that his reasoning had matched hers. "That's what I thought, too. One that they nearly got away with."

Reed slapped one gloved fist into the palm of his hand.

"The false Alexander appears to make a sensation and prove that they have the upper hand among the ton. A devilishly good plan. I wonder whose it was? Lady Jersey? No, the link to Russia is unmistakable. It is the Countess Lieven's handiwork, or I'll go bail. By Jupiter, once the word gets out about this, they shan't be able to hold their heads up anywhere. Trying to pull the wool over the ton's eyes."

"What are you going to do?" Vivian asked.

His blue eyes glittered dangerously. "I am going to pay a call on a Patroness or two."

"May I come with you?" she asked.

"Certainly not. I cannot take you there unescorted."

She sighed. "All these English conventions are most tiresome. Very well. I shall stop at Fanchon's and ask Rory to come with us. Will that do?"

"Yes, but what about your appointment with Fanchon?"

"I only needed to pick up a new dress. Lady Edwina can bring it back."

"Very well, but let's get started. We have several calls to make."

"Mr. Reed and the Misses Spalding, ma'am."

As her butler announced her visitors, Lady Jersey looked up, turning nearly the colour of the purple fringe she was knotting.

"Reed! What are you doing here?" she demanded, before realizing that she had just broken her own edict not to speak to him. But of course it was nearly impossible not to speak to someone who was standing under her own roof.

"Came to have a little chat, my lady," he replied easily. "You are acquainted with Miss Vivian Spalding and Miss Aurora Spalding?"

"Er, yes." The Patroness by now had gathered her wits about her. "But I have nothing to say to any of you. And nothing you may say will be of interest to me."

"Not even if I say it in Russian?" he quizzed. The three of them remained standing, since no invitation to be seated had been given.

Lady Jersey glanced at him. "What do you mean, Russian?"

"I have cut my wisdoms," Reed said in his affable way. "Whose idea was it? Not yours, I'm sure. You have too much sense. And Maria Sefton, dear soul that she is, doesn't have too much in the old cockloft. Mrs. Drummond Burrell doesn't do much except moralize, which leaves either the Princess Esterhazy or the Countess. And since the Countess is Russian, I would suspect the scheme is hers. Am I right?"

"Reed, are you daft? You are not making a mite of sense."

"Not as daft as all of you," he said, inhaling a pinch of snuff, "if you think that you can pass off an impostor as the Tsar."

"Impostor? *You* are queer in the cockloft! Alexander himself is coming to Almack's on Wednesday."

"No, Sally. Three weeks ago Alexander was summoned from India back to St. Petersburg." He glanced over at Vivian, who willingly picked up the narrative.

"The Earl of Atwater received a communication from Lord Montcalm, who is with the Viceroy in India," she explained. "Alexander was called back to St. Petersburg from India."

"But he can't be in St. Petersburg." Lady Jersey rose, letting drop the forgotten fringe. "He is expected here tomorrow. If he doesn't show up..." She paled.

"And if he does show up, he will be much scrutinized to see if he is the real Alexander."

"I see what you are trying to do," Lady Jersey said in a rallying tone. "This is a hoax to disconcert us because your tournament is in disarray."

"My tournament may be in disarray, but it shall be nothing compared to what Almack's will look like when the Tsar doesn't appear. I do wonder who the bogus Alexander is. One of the countess's Russian friends? A relation?"

"She wouldn't—" Lady Jersey paused as she thought of the countess's very superior smile earlier in the week. She looked up at Reed. "What would you have us do?"

"CANCEL ALMACK'S!" Countess Lieven's blue eyes flashed magnificently at the other Patronesses gathered about her. "What sort of addled notion is that?"

"As addled as your notion of trying to pass a bogus Alexander off on the ton," Lady Jersey retorted.

The countess's hand jerked convulsively as she reached for her fan, but she made a swift recovery. "What do you mean, bogus Alexander?"

"Oh, don't peel eggs with us," Lady Jersey exhorted. "Alexander was on his way to St. Petersburg three weeks ago. Who were you going to get to impersonate him on Wednesday?"

The countess fanned her flushed cheeks. "You are not making a particle of sense."

"All I know is that if Alexander appears on Wednesday, he'd better be the genuine article. The gentlemen will be primed to ask him a few military questions."

"Why would they?" the countess demanded. Klaus was a slow top and knew nothing whatever about military strategy.

"Because they will suspect him of not being the Tsar!" Lady Jersey said.

"They could not suspect," the countess murmured.

Seated closest to the countess, Mrs. Burrell lifted an imperious eyebrow.

"Then this outrageous story is true?" Princess Esterhazy asked in her sharp way.

The countess fanned herself more rapidly, remaining silent.

"Why did you say Alexander was coming?" Lady Sefton asked, her usually placid face now twisted with anxiety.

"Because we had to have the room filled again," the countess replied testily. "And it still will be. All we need do is act as though Klaus *is* Alexander."

"Klaus?" Lady Sefton recoiled in the liveliest horror. "Do you mean your blockish cousin, Klaus, the one who cannot enter a room without tripping over his own feet?"

"He bears a striking resemblance to Alexander."

"The resemblance stops at the nose," Lady Jersey said. "Any time he attempts to speak—"

"He shan't speak. He'll appear and dance with me and be on his way."

"That might have worked earlier, but it can't any longer!" Lady Sefton said flatly. "Reed knows. As do the Spaldings. Lord Atwater has a letter stating that Alexander was returning to St. Petersburg, and he could not possibly make the trip from Russia to London in so short a time. We shall be the laughing stock of the ton if we try to pass of Klaus as Alexander. Reed has issued an ultimatum."

The countess sniffed. "He dares to issue ultimatums to us?"

"Would you rather we bring on the bogus Alexander and he be exposed as a fake in front of everyone in the ton?" the princess asked.

A collective shudder ran through the ladies.

"What is his ultimatum?" the countess asked.

Lady Jersey cleared her throat. "That we cancel the meeting at Almack's," she announced.

"Cancel? Preposterous. Who does he think he is?"

"I think we should do as he asks," Lady Sefton said.

"Maria!"

"We cannot produce the bogus Alexander now, can we? And if we hold the Assembly without Alexander, we shan't be able to hold our heads up."

"Bosh," the countess scoffed. "You are turning cat in the pan over the merest threat."

"There's more," Lady Jersey said somberly. "Reed warned that another club could always be opened to rival Almack's."

"Another club?" Princess Esterhazy pursed her lips.

"Clubs have been formed before. We have no reason to be alarmed," Mrs. Burrell clucked.

"If the ton flocks to that club and not ours we shall," Lady Jersey pointed out. "And what will that make us if it comes to pass?"

The five exchanged stricken looks. The time had come for drastic action.

"Who would go to such a club?" the countess wondered aloud.

"Trawley and Reed."

"They speak for the gentlemen, not the ladies."

"Their American friend, Miss Spalding, would go."

Mrs. Burrell sighed. "It would be a novelty—one that we can't afford to let exist."

"How do we prevent such a thing from happening?" the countess demanded.

"We cancel Assembly as Reed demands."

"But what reason can we give?"

"I don't know. Invent one," Mrs. Burrell said, flustered. "I am not the needlewitted one."

"And next week, what do we do then?" the countess asked.

"I think," Lady Jersey replied in measured tones, "that we ought to cancel Assembly for the rest of the Season. There are only two weeks remaining."

"Then you are as good as cancelling the Season."

"We can claim that the weather has been so sultry of late that we wish to go to the seashore."

"I loathe the sea!" the countess pouted.

"Then go to the country!" came the tart rejoinder. "This is all your doing."

"If we stand together no one will discover the cheat."

"Do you think Klaus can withstand close scrutiny?" Lady Jersey asked.

As though to demonstrate the unlikelihood of that, Klaus entered the room just then.

"Cousin, about this uniform," he said, halting when he saw she had company. "Oh, I beg your pardon." He bowed over the princess's hand, almost tripping on his feet as he did so, and hardly bearing himself like the most gallant monarch in all the world.

"Scarlet fever," Countess Lieven said. "I shall have the scarlet fever."

CHAPTER TWELVE

DUE TO A SUDDEN OUTBREAK of scarlet fever in London the Wednesday Assembly was cancelled for the rest of the Season. The Patronesses scattered to the sea and country posthaste, leaving behind London hostesses whose own scheduled balls and routs now went by the board. Many a mother with a marriageable daughter succumbed to the vapours or in their private rooms engaged in temper tantrums. However, no amount of tears could change what had happened. If the Patronesses had all left London, then the Season must be over.

Holland covers were hastily draped on furniture, and last-minute manoeuvering took place to find a sea resort. Everyone knew that only shabby genteels remained in London after a Season.

The swift decline of the Patronesses pleased Vivian, but she was also unnerved at this tangible evidence of Reed's power. Clearly he was not a gentleman to be trifled with.

With Almack's deserted on Wednesday evening—Alexander, it was claimed, had made a hasty change in his plans—Reed's tournament was a resounding success, with the Marquis of Ludwin emerging the eventual victor. Vivian wished to see the tournament, but remembering the brouhaha that had arisen last week when she and Rory had disguised themselves, she was not about to tempt Fate twice. If the cheat were discovered Rory might have to betroth herself quickly to some nearby gentleman. And at the moment Vivian had more than enough betrothals to worry about.

The first to catch her eye was the announcement of her own to Trawley. Lady Edwina had dispatched a notice to the *Gazette*, a fact that took Vivian quite by surprise.

"All betrothals are announced in the *Gazette*," Rory's aunt explained when Vivian approached her about the matter. "It is the English way."

The second betrothal to concern Vivian appeared in the same column as her own, announcing the coming nuptials between Miss Astrid Long and Mr. Clive. The lines of print blurred for a moment as Vivian struggled with an odd emotion in her own breast. She later diagnosed the feeling as hope.

The third betrothal of interest was one which had not yet appeared in print, namely that between Miss Peabody and the Marquis of Ludwin. And for this glaring omission she blamed Reed, who she felt very sure had done nothing to keep Miss Peabody fixed in the mind of the marquis.

"Not doing anything to effect the match?" Reed demanded when she put this charge to him on Thursday morning in the blue drawingroom. "Unfair, Miss Spalding. Quite the opposite. I am getting to be a dead bore on the topic of Miss Peabody."

She passed him a cup of Bohea tea. "Perhaps you do not praise her enough."

He snorted. "I have sung a veritable chorus of praise to her beauty and her gentle nature. Any more and I would drive my friends mad. As it is, even Nigel does not remain long in the room when I get started on the beautiful Miss Peabody. I've done my part."

"Then why hasn't it taken effect?" she demanded after a sip of the fragrant tea.

Reed leaned back in the curricle chair.

"Your American impatience betrays you yet again. We English do not rush in where angels fear to tread, particularly into marriages. Ludwin will be landed."

"How can you be so sure?"

"I have only to mention Miss Peabody, and the fellow turns into a mooncalf. Cupid has aimed his arrows well." He gave a derisive laugh.

Vivian eyed him as he sat looking rather satisfied with himself. "You are not very romantic, Mr. Reed. But then you told me that you have never felt Cupid's arrow yourself."

"Never," he averred. "I don't believe in such romantic bibble-babble. A marriage should be contracted soberly, without worrying about a *grande passion*."

"Such as the one to come between Mr. Clive and Miss Long?" she asked.

"Well, yes," he said, fortifying himself with a pinch of snuff. "Odd to have my place filled by that fop, Clive."

"Do you plan to meet him at Paddington Green?"

He inhaled the snuff a tad too vigorously and began to sneeze.

"Meet him at Paddington?" he said when he could speak.

"Yes. He's stolen a march on you with Miss Long."

"You are a bloodthirsty chit, aren't you?" he remarked. "No, by heaven, I'm not going to duel with the fellow. If he wants Astrid, he's welcome to her. I should dispatch a wedding present to her and Clive to show that there is no animosity. What do you think they will like?"

"Perhaps an ornament for their residence?"

He shook his head. "Astrid doesn't think twice about furniture or painting." He snapped his fingers. "I have it, a matching set of swans. They can pluck the feathers if they like."

Despite her best attempt to keep a straight face, Vivian laughed. Then she declared, "Odious creature, I wish you will not mention feathers to me!"

"You told me once that I am forbidden to mention your clothing to you, must I now add feathers to that list?" he protested with mischievous eyes. "I hope you will leave me some topics of conversation to pursue with you, Miss Spalding."

"Don't be absurd. You may speak to me about my clothing if you wish," she said, wondering what he would say about the blue morning dress she wore.

He shook his head firmly. "I think not."

"Why not? Do you think me hideously frumpy?"

"Not at all hideous, and far from frumpy," he said with a smile. "What I should like to praise—" To her great annoyance he left the sentence unfinished because Viscount Trawley strolled in.

"Ah, George, come to call on Miss Spalding?" Reed enquired with an autocratic lift of his brow.

"Yes, I have," the viscount said, brandishing a copy of the *Gazette*. "Miss Spalding, have you seen this issue? There is a notice about our engagement. I thought we'd agreed—"

"I know that your mother wanted to do it," Vivian said hastily, determined not to have him reveal to Reed their bogus engagement, "but Lady Edwina went ahead and did it herself."

"I wish she hadn't. It makes things deuced difficult."

"Yes, your mother will undoubtedly be displeased. I rely on you to coax her out of the hips. And now I recall we are driving this morning to Hampton Court maze, are we not?"

He looked at her with complete befuddlement. "We are?"

She laughed. "Come, my lord, surely because we are engaged now you have not forgot me," she said rallyingly.

"No, I beg pardon. Abominable memory," Trawley said. "Hampton Court, you say?"

Reed rose languidly.

"I won't delay you from your drive with Trawley," he said to Vivian. "I am myself late for an appointment with Gentleman Jackson."

"Did we really have an appointment to drive today?" Trawley asked after they were alone. "I know my memory is shockingly bad."

"No, we didn't. But I had to find a way of getting time alone with you."

"Oh?" He peered at his companion with some consternation.

"You must never tell Reed the truth about our engagement."

"Why not?" Reading the notice in the *Gazette* had sobered the viscount considerably. Was Miss Spalding bent on an elaborate plot to lure him to St. George's, Hanover Square?

"Because I'd rather he not know," Vivian said lamely. "He believes no one in his right mind would marry me."

"Reed doesn't think that," Trawley protested.

"I assure you he does. I assume that he thinks Rory, being younger, could abandon her hoydenish American ways and make some gentleman a dutiful wife, but it is too late for me."

"Has Rory expressed any interest in matrimony?" Trawley asked, frowning.

"No, not at all. And if she did I hope her grandfather would not dispatch an announcement to the *Gazette* prematurely. I do apologize for that, but I had no way of knowing what Lady Edwina was up to. Is our betrothal so inconvenient for you?"

"Inconvenient?" Her choice of word puzzled him.

"I know gentlemen such as yourselves have—pray, what is the term—chères amies? I hope that yours is not too angry with you."

He laughed. "I don't have a chère amie at the moment."

"Really? I had thought all gentlemen did. Even the Royal Dukes. Doesn't Reed?" she asked, then wondered what had possessed her to ask such a freakish question. Reed's chères amies were none of her business.

"To my knowledge, no," Trawley said now.

"Not ever?"

"That might be doing it too brown," the viscount said. "But Lucian is not thick in the muslin company. On the other hand he's not a monk, either. Have you thought how much longer you will be in London? The Season is over now that the Patronesses have left."

This query brought to mind her own reluctance to think about her future in Philadelphia. London ways were strange, but she had grown fond of some of the people here.

"I'm not sure exactly what we will do," she said, staring down into the palms of her hands as though she were a gypsy blessed with second sight. "I had planned to return to America, remember."

"You can certainly delay your departure a week or two," he pointed out. "It will take that long to secure passage. May I make a suggestion? My estate is in Derbyshire, as is Lord Atwater's. Since he has told me about his plan to remove there in the summer, may I invite you to Trawle? Your sister may enjoy it, too. I have several horses that are tame creatures and the weather is generally pleasant."

"That's kind of you."

"And of course my mother will be in attendance."

"Your mother?"

His dark eyes glinted with amusement. "Yes, Miss Spalding. Even rakes have mothers. She is sure to have read the announcement in the *Gazette,* so I think I should let her have a look at you. When you have returned to America I shall tell her the truth."

"When I return to America," Vivian murmured softly. She felt her throat catch at the idea of returning to her native soil. She was still sitting in the drawingroom when Rory came in a half hour later and demanded to know why she hadn't been informed that Trawley had come and gone.

"I didn't know you wished particularly to see him," Vivian said.

"I didn't *particularly* wish to see him," Rory said. "I just wished to see him, that's all." She flounced out of the room, leaving Vivian to wonder just what was in her sister's mind.

LATER THAT AFTERNOON as Reed climbed the steps to White's, he encountered the Marquis Ludwin.

"Good day to you, Ludwin," he remarked genially. "You slept the sleep of the victorious, I presume."

Ludwin's lips spread wide in a smile. "Indeed, I have," he answered. "A pity the tournament is over."

"You can always put your championship to the test again," Reed pointed out.

The marquis shook his head ruefully. "It is so new to me that I am loath to put it up so soon. Perhaps in a month's time."

"By then most of our companions will be in the country. What are your plans for the summer?" Reed asked as they entered White's together.

"Haven't made them yet," the marquis said.

"Brighton is always enjoyable. But always expensive and crowded. Will Miss Peabody be off to the country this summer?"

Ludwin took this change of topic in stride. "I don't know."

"I should hate to think that she will be soon gone. Rarely have I seen anyone distinguish London with her grace and easy ways. What say you, Ludwin?"

"I quite agree, of course," the marquis replied politely.

"A veritable paragon among women."

The two gentlemen entered the readingroom and encountered that paragon's father, who was just about to settle back with a copy of the *Racing News*. The sight of the marquis entering brought to Peabody's mind his daughter's tearful behaviour of late.

Mr. Peabody was a blunt man, a quality exacerbated by the debts he owed. He knew very well he had produced a diamond of the first water in his daughter, and he was quite willing to use that piece of good luck to solve his own predicament.

"Ah, Lord Ludwin," he boomed heartily. "Been meaning to have a word with you, my lord."

"Mr. Peabody, good day. You know Mr. Reed, do you not?"

The two men exchanged bows.

"How is your lovely daughter, Mr. Peabody?" Reed enquired.

"Crying her pretty eyes out because of the cancellation of the Season," Mr. Peabody replied with his usual frankness. "The Patronesses *would* make micefeet of everything! I need to know if you have any interest in my daughter, Ludwin, for if you do I'd like you to speak up and tell me your intentions. If you don't, why then I can get on with marrying her off to someone else."

"My dear sir..." the marquis began, astonished at such plain speaking.

Reed polished a quizzing glass. What Mr. Peabody lacked for in funds he certainly made up with forthrightness. Perhaps he should follow Peabody's lead and nudge Ludwin himself.

"Mr. Peabody is right, Ludwin. You have kept poor Miss Peabody on tenterhooks long enough. Will you have her or won't you? There are many in the ton who would snatch her up."

White-faced, the marquis turned from his friend.

"Sweetest-natured girl I know," Reed went on. "Make any man a fine wife. Cheerful..."

"Stop!" the marquis exclaimed. "You need say no more, sir."

"I thought not," Reed said with a little smile.

The marquis turned to Mr. Peabody. "Here is the person who is most desirous of marrying your daughter! I leave it to the two of you to thrash out the details of his attachment." He then turned and swiftly quitted the reading-room.

If the marquis had suddenly announced his plan to join the exiled Napoleon on his island, Reed could not have been more astonished.

While he gaped for words, Mr. Peabody rubbed his palms together.

"So you are thoroughly besotted with my daughter, are you?" he asked.

Reed made a feeble attempt to gather his wits. "Yes, I mean, no. I mean..."

The older man laughed indulgently. "Ta, la, man. I know how it is when one is in the throes of a *grande passion*. As long as I know your attentions are honourable I shan't stand in your way. When do you plan to speak for her?"

Reed's collar points felt tight enough to squeeze the air from his body. "Speak for her? Your daughter? Mr. Peabody, pray don't misunderstand me. I think Miss Peabody a veritable paragon, but I never once dreamed of offering for her."

"I know the feeling," Mr. Peabody replied, with a sympathetic nod. "Men without titles often are overlooked, are we not? But I'm not afraid to take a man without a title for my daughter. Lord Steiker made me an offer for her, and I thought of marrying her to him if Ludwin didn't come up to scratch."

"But Steiker is so old!"

"Just five-and-sixty," Mr. Peabody said. "And you needn't protest too vehemently about Steiker. I won't marry Emily to him. Not when there is a sensible fellow like you who wants her."

Reed felt the noose tightening about his neck. He had no wish to marry the Peabody chit. But could he really stand by and watch her wed Steiker, whose reputation with females was shabby indeed?

"Mr. Peabody—" he began attempting once more to make sense of this coil.

"Emily will be agreeable. And my wife will be cast in alt. She was all atwitter that the end of the Season had come so abruptly, fearing that Emily would be left on the shelf. We should have the announcement in the *Gazette* by week's end."

STILL REELING from the shock of finding himself suddenly affianced to Miss Peabody, Reed lost no time in confiding the enormity of what had just transpired to Vivian. If he had expected a sympathetic audience to his plight, he was sorely mistaken.

"I should have known that you would make a bumblebroth of all this," Vivian declared, pacing back and forth in the music room.

"I merely performed a favour for you."

Vivian stopped in midstride and glared at him. "Forgive me, Mr. Reed. I am not used to London ways, but when exactly did I ever ask you to betroth yourself to Miss Peabody?"

"I didn't betroth myself. Her father did it for me." Reed spoke through gritted teeth.

"I cannot believe that Mr. Peabody would take it upon himself to betroth his daughter to you on a whim."

"It wasn't a whim. It was Ludwin's doing."

She threw up her hands. "Do you mean Ludwin was present? Do you mean he did not speak for Miss Peabody on his own behalf?"

"No. He thrust me into the muddle, saying that I was thoroughly besotted with her. And that is your fault."

"It's my fault that you are thoroughly besotted with Miss Peabody?" Vivian demanded, out of patience with these obstacles in her plan to bring the marquis and Miss Peabody together.

"I am not besotted with anyone!" he thundered. "I followed your orders to sing Miss Peabody's praises at every opportunity. So it's no wonder Ludwin thought I was top over tail in love with the chit."

"Why didn't you tell Mr. Peabody that you didn't wish to marry his daughter?"

"I tried to, but then he told me he was entertaining Lord Steiker's suit. He's a loose screw. I couldn't just leave Miss Peabody to the likes of him."

"Very noble of you."

He glared at her. "Why don't you help me instead of just making cutting remarks?"

She sighed and dropped into a chair. "Actually, we needn't make this a Cheltenham tragedy. Miss Peabody loves Lord Ludwin. She will undoubtedly reject your suit."

This possibility had never entered Reed's head. Along with a sudden flood of relief he felt a flicker of annoyance.

"Do you really think that possible?" he asked, looking down his nose at Vivian.

Presented with this new evidence of his arrogance, Vivian felt tempted to let him suffer.

"You are not the only eligible in London," she pointed out. "Ludwin eclipses you in rank and is much younger than you."

"What has his lack of years to do with anything?" he demanded. "I am two-and-thirty, hardly in my dotage. I believe some ladies prefer maturity in gentlemen."

"Some do," she conceded. "Others like the agility of youth."

He snorted. "I'm not Methuselah yet," he declared. "I hope you are right that Miss Peabody is besotted with Nigel, for I am set to make my offer to her this week."

"What a pity I shan't be here to hear about your proposal. We leave for Derbyshire tomorrow."

"Derbyshire? What the devil is in Derbyshire?"

"Trawley's country seat."

Reed forgot all about his impending engagement and faced the reality of hers to Trawley.

"He's taking you home to meet his mother?"

"Yes," she said. "Rory comes with me. Trawley promised to mount us, and she is looking forward to riding."

"And what of you?"

"I will ride, too."

"You are a notable horsewoman?"

"Hardly that. But I shall try and amuse myself and stay out of trouble."

Reed's eyes held an ironic gleam. "Stay out of trouble? I deem that an impossibility where you are concerned, Miss Spalding. In your two weeks here in London you've caused the cancellation of the Season!"

"Too harsh. You had something to do with it."

"If you had not arrived in London I would never have crossed swords with the Patronesses."

That was true, she admitted.

"Do you have plans for the summer?" She turned the question to him.

"I will be visiting friends. Perhaps in Cornwall."

"Then this might be goodbye," she said, holding out her hand.

He stared at it for a moment.

"Your American impatience to be rid of me," he said.

She swallowed the lump in her throat. She wasn't at all eager to be rid of him.

"Goodbye, Mr. Reed."

He took her small hand in his large one, holding it for a moment. "I shan't say goodbye to you," he retorted, "but *au revoir*, which is French for 'until we see each other again.' Which I am confident we shall." He kissed her hand softly, and she felt a sudden jolt. "Now you must say *au revoir* back to me."

"*Au revoir,*" she said, smiling through a haze which she realized later was tears.

But why was she crying? Reed was a frivolous fribble, even though of late she had begun to revise that opinion of him. When she first clapped eyes on him she'd thought him a veritable tulip, but by now she was well aware that he wore his fashionable clothing with quiet elegance that others in the ton would do well to emulate.

She wiped her eyes, scolded herself for being a goose, and told herself that it was a very good thing that she was going back to America, a statement that she stoutly repeated to herself in the vain hope that she would grow to believe it.

CHAPTER THIRTEEN

LADY EDWINA WARMLY approved Vivian's plans to remove to Derbyshire.

"Of course you must go to Trawle," she declared, one silver curl peeping out from under a cap as she helped Vivian sort through the wardrobe. "You must meet Lady Trawley. He will accompany you, I take it?"

"Yes. And Rory comes with us, too."

"Good. Charles will follow you in a sennight."

Vivian smoothed the blue walking dress on the bed. "And what about you, ma'am?"

Lady Edwina gave a rueful smile. "I will be visiting my sister in York. There is no getting out of the visit. She was most insistent."

"Do you have many relations, ma'am?"

"Too many," Lady Edwina said with a heartfelt sigh.

Vivian picked up one of the ball gowns that she had never used. "Might you have any relations in Cornwall?"

"Good heavens, child. What puts Cornwall in your mind?"

"Mr. Reed mentioned that he had friends there."

"I suppose he does. Lucian has scores of friends." Lady Edwina folded a pelisse. "I do hope Trawley sends his travel chaise so you won't be jolted all over the road in a Mail Coach."

The viscount did indeed send his chaise for them the next morning, and as the servants loaded the Spaldings' portmanteaux Lady Edwina called out: "Rory, where are you?"

"Here I am, Aunt," Rory said, coming down the stairs in a furious clatter. "Vivian, do hurry. Lord Trawley is here and has the most splendid carriage. Oh, Aunt, I shall miss you!" She flung her arms about Lady Edwina and then gave her grandfather a fierce hug.

Vivian's parting with the earl and his sister was less demonstrative but just as deeply felt. In good conscience she did not know when she would see them next, and the two had been so kind. Only recently had she come to realize how bold had been her journey with Rory across the Atlantic. The two sisters could have easily met with a repulse from Lord Atwater, but instead he had extended his hospitality and protection.

"You will take care of them, won't you?" the earl asked Trawley.

"I will handle them as carefully as a pair of priceless Ming vases."

"A vase!" Rory hooted. "We are not so fragile, are we, Vivian?"

"No, indeed," she said, trying to fall in with the spirit of the journey.

Luckily her companions were in a garrulous mood and she amused herself with their chatter as the carriage swung from London into Derbyshire. She felt herself nodding off to sleep at one point, and when she heard her name called and her shoulder shaken she came awake.

"Reed?" she asked groggily as her eyes attempted to focus on the man in front of her.

"It's Trawley, Viv!" Rory exclaimed.

"Oh, I beg pardon. Why are we stopping?"

"To have something to eat," the viscount explained. "Rory's famished, and I'm parched."

He handed them down and the three made their way into a private parlour of the posting house. Over a roasted chicken and three different side dishes, Trawley explained that his mother was an invalid due to an injury suffered years ago in a carriage accident.

"The poor lady!" Rory said with quick sympathy. "How does she get about?"

"Her household of servants would cheerfully slay anyone who touched a hair on her head," he said. "So she goes on very well indeed."

NEVERTHELESS EVEN Trawley was surprised to find her waiting belowstairs for them when they arrived at Trawle.

"Mama, you should not have come down!" the viscount scolded, pecking her on a powdered cheek. She clasped his hand in hers.

"Now, if you have come home to pinch and scold me, George, I shall send you packing," she retorted with a smile. "I have been on pins and needles to meet my future daughter-in-law, and you shan't keep me from her."

"In truth, I wouldn't," he said with a smile. "For I am eager to have you meet her and her sister."

"Good. Now where are they?"

He laughed. "I left them in the carriage. They are worn down by the trip, poor creatures, and have fallen asleep in the carriage. But I shall awaken them—"

"You shall do no such thing," she contradicted. "Let them rest. This will give you time to tell me how comes it that you are engaged in so swift a fashion."

He took the chair next to hers in the sittingroom, wondering where to begin.

"You are surprised?" he hazarded a guess.

"Happily so," she assured him. "I had not supposed you to be the marrying kind."

He laughed. "That was before I met the Spalding sisters. I vow between the two of them they have quite set London on its ear. Did you hear that the Patronesses cancelled Assembly?"

"That wasn't their doing, was it?"

"Partly."

"Stop being so gudgeonish, George, and tell me more."

Trawley needed no coaxing and was soon telling his mother about the charming Spalding sisters. Lady Trawley's brow knit a little in puzzlement. The startling betrothal announcement in the *Gazette* linked her son with Miss Vivian Spalding, but he seemed to be spending more time detailing the charms of Aurora Spalding.

"How old is she?" the viscountess asked now.

"Eighteen."

"You are marrying someone practically out of the schoolroom!"

"Oh, no. You meant Vivian. She's twenty-one, I believe. Rory is eighteen. And she's never been in the schoolroom, she says. Vivian has always been her teacher."

Lady Trawley surreptitiously watched as her son stretched out his top boots towards the fire. "Are you fond of Vivian, George?"

"Er, yes..."

"And her sister?"

"Rory? Well, of course, Mama." He looked at her closely. "That goes without saying."

"Does it, indeed?"

A few minutes later Lady Trawley had the opportunity to observe for herself the Spalding sisters after they awakened and were presented to her. Rory, smothering a yawn and looking like a tiny kitten, she quite took to her heart, and she was also prepared to like Vivian, who apologized for their rag manners in falling asleep in the carriage and keeping her waiting.

The afternoon passed amicably. After a wash and a short rest, the Spalding sisters were revived enough to walk about in the Shakespeare gardens with Trawley, and when Vivian spied his mother sitting under a lime tree with a copy of Byron, she strolled over to join her.

"Are you enjoying your walk, Miss Spalding?" Lady Trawley asked.

"Oh, yes. You have so many roses, ma'am, and the scent is heavenly."

"They are my pride and joy, next to my son, of course. Now, you must tell me all the latest on-dits in London."

"I would do so willingly, but I don't quite know—"

"What is fit for a decrepit old lady's ears?"

"No!" she said. Old was not how she would have described the viscountess. True, there were flecks of silver in the dark hair, but the blue eyes were alive and twinkling with laughter. "I just don't know what is gossip or who is worthy of gossip."

"Good. You would be surprised at those who because of my injury think they must tell me morally uplifting stories." A gleam like her son's danced in her eyes. "I'd as lief have unworthy tales to speculate upon."

Vivian laughed.

"George's good friend, Lucian Reed—how does he go on?"

"Quite well, ma'am," Vivian said, surprised that out of all the people in London Lady Trawley should single out Reed.

"What happened between him and Astrid Long? I saw her name linked with that idiotish fop, Mr. Clive."

"Actually, that was partly my doing."

"Yours?" Lady Trawley lifted an eyebrow, clearly intrigued.

"It all started with feathers..."

By the end of the recitation Lady Trawley was in whoops, and Vivian was quite worried about her.

"No, not my hartshorn, just a glass of water," the viscountess said, gesturing to a nearby pitcher on a garden stool.

Vivian brought her a glass.

"My dear, I congratulate you," the older woman said when she could speak. "To have broken up Reed and Astrid Long is quite an accomplishment. He shall thank you for it some day."

"Do you know him well, ma'am?"

"I knew his father. He was a wastrel and a gambler despite his charm."

The sound of laughter brought an end to her reminiscences as Rory and Trawley approached. Dressed in a sprig muslin dress, Rory carried a huge bouquet of red and yellow roses.

"No more," Rory laughed. "Look, Viv, Trawley has cut so many that his gardener is sure to send in his notice."

"They are lovely," Vivian said, bending her head to inhale their fragrance.

Rory plucked one out and handed it to her. "For you." She turned to Lady Trawley. "For you, ma'am. Trawley, I must arrange these in a vase."

"You see how I am ordered about," he told his mother in mock umbrage before going into the house with Rory.

"Your sister is charming," Lady Trawley said, sitting back with Vivian.

"Oh, yes, everyone loves Rory," Vivian said, glad that Lady Trawley had not taken offence at Rory's behaviour. Far from being offended, the viscountess was intrigued to see her son practically wrapped around the thumb of any female, let alone a potential sister-in-law. She could fully understand if it had been Vivian whose every wish he sought to fulfil, but although he was a dutiful host to Vivian, it seemed that he paid most of his attention to Rory. As the days progressed, Lady Trawley still did not quite know what to make of it.

"TRAWLEY'S MOTHER likes you," Vivian said to her sister as they prepared for bed one night.

The evening had been a quiet one, with all four playing whist, which the viscountess particularly enjoyed.

"She is a pet," Rory said, brushing her hair. "So different from Mama. Lady Trawley never complains even though she must be in pain."

"Yes," Vivian murmured.

Rory threw her a sidelong glance. "Vivian, this engagement between you and Trawley is a hum, isn't it?"

"You know that it is."

"Yes, but the announcement appeared in the *Gazette* and you are visiting his mother, and Grandfather thinks—" she broke off, on the verge of tears.

"Good heavens, Rory!" Vivian turned her sister's face towards her. "You love Trawley, don't you?" she asked, correctly deducing the reason for Rory's distress.

"Oh, yes, Viv!" Rory exclaimed, so obviously from the heart that Vivian knew her idyll in the country was at an end.

As she listened to Rory declare her feelings for the rakish viscount, Vivian knew she must secure her passage to America as soon as possible. Then she could jilt Trawley, who would be free to offer for Rory.

"Don't worry, my dear," she said as she blew the light out by her bed, "the engagement is a hoax, and things will be settled within another week."

Rory breathed a sigh of relief.

Vivian lay back on a goose-down pillow, thinking of the love she saw reflected in the eyes of Rory and Trawley whenever they looked at each other. Unbidden, thoughts of Reed sprang to her mind.

She rolled over on her side and punched the pillow with a fist. *Do stop thinking of him,* she told herself. She would wager a pony that he had not thought of her once in the last sennight.

IN THIS INSTANCE, however, Vivian would have been entirely wrong. Reed had been doing considerable thinking about her, but his thoughts dwelt on mayhem rather than romance.

On the same day that she had begun her journey to Derbyshire, he had gone to call on Miss Peabody, secure in the belief that she would throw him over for Ludwin. So he was utterly dumbfounded when she cast her eyes shyly up to his and replied that she would be happy to accept his offer.

"Accept my offer! But you can't!" he expostulated. "Er, that is, I have it on good authority that you're in love with Ludwin. Surely you want to wait until he makes you an offer."

"He won't," she said darkly. "He has forgot all about me. Any tendre I may have nursed for him is at an end. When we marry I shall put all thought of him out of my mind, I assure you of that."

"Marriage!" Reed uttered a silent oath on the head of an unsuspecting Vivian Spalding. It was her fault he was involved in this ridiculous situation. He'd sung the praises of Miss Peabody to the marquis, and see what was the result. He himself was due to march up the aisle of St. George's with her!

He would have argued more vehemently with Miss Peabody, but just then the door to the private room opened and Mrs. Peabody bustled in, to be greeted with the happy news of a prospective son-in-law. The next hour passed in joyful preparation of wedding plans, which had the effect of sending Reed off on an immediate search for Ludwin.

To his shock Reed found Ludwin's residence on Green Street boarded up, and a search for him amid the establishments of London proved fruitless.

"Where the devil could he be?" Reed asked himself as he left word in Manton's and Jackson's.

"Were you talking to me, Reed?" the Earl of Atwater asked as he passed him on the street.

"Oh, Charles. I beg your pardon. No, just woolgathering."

The earl, although not one to dabble in gossip, had heard the rumours that Reed had become engaged to Miss Peabody and had thereupon been seen in some of the notorious gambling hells in London.

"I should be wishing you happy, I have heard."

"Happy?" Reed looked anything but. "Oh, you mean Miss Peabody."

"Yes, of course, Miss Peabody," the earl said. He took Reed by the arm and drew him aside. "You know I don't like to poke my nose into what don't concern me, Lucian. And I know that love has a way of unhinging a gentleman, but I thought I should drop a word in your ear. If you want to gamble, stick to White's or Watier's, even. You'll come to grief in those Greeking establishments."

"Charles!"

"I've seen it happen before. The ones who are so opposed to gambling get a taste of it and that is enough to set them off. Before the night is over they are ditched. Saw it happen to your father."

"My father?"

"He wasn't always a wastrel," the earl said. "You remind me of him. Well, he got a taste of cards and that was his end. I don't want it to be yours."

"It shan't be," Reed assured him. "I've no interest in gaming."

The earl looked sceptical. "Then why are you racketing about in some of the hells?"

"Because I've been trying to find Ludwin. He's my one chance to be free of Miss Peabody."

"Free of her? You just got engaged to her," the earl said, staggered by this display of fickleness in the younger generation of males.

"Yes, I know. But it's not me she wants. It's Ludwin, and I have been searching London to find him. You wouldn't know where he's gone, would you?"

"I don't. But Edwina is a bosom bow to his mother. She might know."

In due course Lady Edwina was questioned, and Reed learned that the marquis had paid a call on his mother, informing her that he was bound for Rouen in France.

There was only one thing to do: go to France and find the marquis and bring him back to wed Miss Peabody.

VIVIAN HAD THOUGHT that it would be a simple task to make plans to return to Philadelphia from Derbyshire, but she soon discovered that the situation was more difficult than she had assumed.

First came the matter of secrecy. She could not divulge to Rory that she was leaving, since she knew the inevitable tears that would result. She might have confided in Trawley, but she wished him not merely to act the part of the astonished, jilted lover but to actually be astonished.

She thought briefly of confiding in his mother, but she knew that the old lady was growing fond of her and might coax her into staying, and that would never do. So she fretted as more days passed and finally she made plans to go into the village to see if she might make some discreet enquiries about passage to America.

Her first opportunity to drive into town came because Trawley's mother wished to return a book that she had borrowed from a friend.

Vivian eagerly volunteered to return the book and then, later, went to the village square, hoping to find some news of a ship bound for America.

She was in luck, for as she neared the square she recognized, sitting at one of the tables, Captain Gouge, who had been in charge of her passage from Philadelphia to London. Surely he would know of a ship back to America.

"Indeed, I do," the captain said. "It's the *Merriman*."

"The same one we sailed over on?"

"Aye, and I am captaining it. We sail out of Bristol next week Tuesday for Boston."

"I know the route," she said. "I would like to book passage for one."

"Your sister?"

"Remains behind in England."

"England not to your taste?" he enquired, twirling his moustache. "Not to mine either, in truth. The passage will be a hundred pounds."

"I can give you ten pounds now," she said, digging into her reticule. "And I shall bring you the other ninety before we sail. Will that do?"

"Yes, Miss Spalding," he said, taking the ten pounds from her.

"What a good thing we happened to meet. I don't know what I would have done otherwise."

And she left, secure in the feeling that her troubles in England would soon be over.

REED STARED THROUGH HIS quizzing glass at the man draped over the coffeeroom table. He had spent a long, arduous week on the most abominable French roads on a quest, and here finally lay his golden fleece: Ludwin, thoroughly foxed.

"Been that way for the past three days," the gat-toothed innkeeper confided.

Reed left the marquis on the table snoring loudly and dispatched the innkeeper to the kitchen to provide the best dinner available, then he seated himself in front of the fire with a tankard of ale and thought back on his last seven days.

He had thought it a simple matter to cross the Channel, find the marquis and prevail upon him to return to Miss Peabody. Crossing the Channel proved to be the simplest of the three tasks he had set himself, even though a storm blew up midway across it.

By the time he had reached France, he was tired and hungry and in no mood to do anything but pack the marquis back to England. Lady Edwina's information about Ludwin's whereabouts proved sadly deficient, and it took Reed several days to track him down to this inn outside Paris.

Reed shot a glance now at the slumbering marquis. His clothes were in disarray, looking as though he had spent all week in them. He could hardly send the marquis back to Miss Peabody looking like that: she might have second thoughts about him. He must delay until Nigel could be tidied up.

The innkeeper entered, carrying several steaming dishes including a beef bourguignon and a hearty apple tart. The smell reminded Reed how long it had been since he had eaten. The food took the edge off his fatigue and bad temper.

"I'll need your best room and one for my friend here," he told the innkeeper.

"We have only one room, a very large one. It has two beds."

Reed glared at the snoring marquis. It would have to do, he supposed.

"By the way, innkeeper, how long are your beds?"

"My beds?" The innkeeper frowned.

"Never mind. I shall find out for myself."

Leaving the innkeeper and a helper to carry the marquis up to the room, Reed finished his dinner. The long trip had taken its toll on him, and he stifled a yawn. Or maybe it was just the French wine. He climbed the stairs to his room and found the marquis already sprawled in one bed.

The bed was not as short as the previous night's lodgings, but Reed could not help yearning for his huge four-poster back in London. By all rights he should be there, sinking into the goose-down mattress, instead of dealing with a hard, narrow cot. Wearily he sat down on the bed. His head spun, no doubt a consequence of the wine he had drunk, and darkness claimed him.

Several hours later the door to Reed's room opened slightly. Two men scurried into the darkness.

"His purse, and be quick about it."

"No cause for alarm. The sleeping draught I gave him will keep him out most of the night."

The other man was searching Reed's pockets. With a cry of glee he found the purse. He shook it and cackled loudly.

" 'Twill be full of gold."

"Give it here," the innkeeper said impatiently. "I marked him for us. Gave him the sleeping draught."

"But I'll take the risk afterwards driving him out in my vehicle and losing him far from here."

The innkeeper counted out the coins. "Here's half. You take him away and that friend he came looking for."

"What, two men to carry? I'll need more than that."

The innkeeper added another coin to the pile. "But no more."

The other robber looked inclined to protest but he gave in, pocketed the coins and with the innkeeper's help pulled Reed to his feet. With luck they could pass him off as yet another Englishman who could not hold his wine.

CHAPTER FOURTEEN

VIVIAN RECOUNTED THE GOLD coins in her hand. Thank heaven she had saved some of the money that her father had given her when she and Rory left America. Impatiently she glanced about her in the village square. Finally, she spotted Captain Gouge hurrying towards her.

"Ah, Miss Spalding, right on time."

"It was very kind of you to meet me here, Captain," Vivian said.

"Where is your sister? Doesn't she wish to see you off?"

Vivian shook her head. Rory would be as surprised as Trawley to get the note she had left. The two of them were on a picnic, and when they returned they would find the note she had propped up on her pillow.

"Is this your carriage?" the captain asked, gesturing at Trawley's vehicle.

"I borrowed it. I shall catch a Mail Coach to Bristol. But I wanted to make sure I had passage aboard your ship."

"Aye, that you have," he said taking out a paper from his coat. She read it through. As captain of the *Merriman*, Gouge had booked one passage for Vivian Spalding. Paid in advance.

"And now the matter of the ninety pounds?"

"Certainly..." Vivian handed him the bag of coins. "The ship sails in forty-eight hours you said, Captain?"

"Aye. You will forgive me if I don't offer you a lift to Bristol with me," the captain said. "But an unescorted lady with a ship's captain..."

"Of course," she said. "I understand. The coach stop is not that far away. I shall reach Bristol in plenty of time for the departure."

"And then it's back to Philadelphia?" he asked in a bluff voice.

Vivian managed a brave smile. "Yes, back to Philadelphia."

NEARLY TWENTY-FOUR HOURS later, Vivian stumbled from a Mail Coach and out onto the darkened streets of Bristol. The journey had been as expected. She'd been jolted and jarred until her temples throbbed.

She was also ravenous. A farmer's wife had shared her cheese and bread, but that had been very early in the trip.

Philadelphia. She thought of that city now as she walked towards a posting house in search of breakfast. Once Philadelphia was home; now it was just a place from her past.

Odd to think she had come to England aboard the *Merriman* and would be sailing back to America on the same ship. Did things never change? she wondered.

Later that afternoon she realized just how much things had changed as she stared in dismay at the empty slip along the Bristol waterfront. The *Merriman* was nowhere in sight.

"The *Merriman*," she said quickly to one of the sailors on a nearby boat. "Where is it?"

"Bound for Boston, miss."

"But it can't be. It sails this Tuesday. The captain told me so himself."

The sailor squinted at her. "What captain is that?"

"Captain Gouge."

The sailor spat. "That rogue."

"Rogue?"

"Aye... he had a rum bit of luck. Thievery, pure and simple. So they took the ship away from him. Sorry, miss, if you're wanting passage to America you'll have to wait until next week when the *Hoover* sails."

"I can't wait...." Vivian's head throbbed. This was a nightmare. All her plans for naught. She walked away, feeling close to despair. She had no passage to America and not enough money to pay for her way on the next ship. What should she do? She couldn't return to Trawle. The note she had left behind for the viscount and Rory made clear her plan of action. To reappear now would spoil everything for Rory and the viscount, who might again take it in his head to do the honourable thing and marry Vivian.

She heaved a despairing sigh and glanced over at another, much smaller boat loading passengers.

"Where is that one going?" she asked a passer-by.

"To Dieppe, miss."

France wasn't America, but at least it wasn't England. She pulled out the last coin in her bag. Maybe with luck she could find a future in France.

COMING AWAKE IN THE HARSH sunlight, Reed thought he was still asleep as he turned on the uncomfortable cot. But this was not a cot, but earth, and damp earth at that. He brought his hand up to his forehead, shielding his eyes against the rays which had awakened him.

The marquis's vigorous shaking had helped to rouse Reed from the draught-induced slumber. He sat up, squinting at Ludwin, who sat back on his own heels.

"Of all the people in Christendom I expected to see here, you are the last, Reed," the marquis declared.

Reed grunted a reply. His tongue felt thick and useless.

"What are you doing here?" Ludwin went on.

"If by here you mean this very spot, I don't know," came the reply as Reed stood and stretched his legs. "I was at that vile inn you were frequenting and had gone to bed..." He broke off and conducted a rapid search of his pockets. As he had feared, his roll of notes was gone.

"Blast!"

"Victim of a highwayman, if would appear," Ludwin observed sagely.

"Not a highwayman, a thieving innkeeper. And he'll not get away with it."

"I think he has been getting away with it for considerable time," the marquis countered, taking in stride the loss of Reed's purse. "My pockets were to let after a week at his inn," he explained. "I can't think why he deposited me in so disreputable a fashion out here in the cold and wet. You, I might see, being so newly arrived with a fat purse—"

"Where the devil are we?" Reed asked, cutting short this litany of complaints.

"In France, I think.... This sun is most unlike England."

"But where in France?"

"I don't know," the marquis said affably. "My geography was always deploringly bad. Not as bad as my Latin..."

Adjured by Reed to be quiet and see what valuables they possessed, the marquis conducted a hasty inventory of his person. Although neither had any broken bones, they were dirty and penniless. In addition to their missing purses, the thieves had taken their rings and fobs and watches and their coats.

"We have to get back to England somehow," Reed declared.

"Speak for yourself. I am in no hurry to return to England."

"You prefer a life as a pauper in France?"

Ludwin kicked a stone with the toe of his boot. "Doesn't make any difference."

"Can you speak any French?"

"Not worth mentioning," the marquis said cheerfully.

"Then you'll go mad here."

"You needn't concern yourself with me, Reed," Ludwin said, cutting up stiff.

"Take a damper. You are a concern to me, particularly since I have come to take you back to that Peabody chit."

The marquis's jaw tightened. "Don't taunt me, blast you. I know very well *you* love Emily."

"No, I don't."

"You don't?" Ludwin frowned. "Then why were you always telling me how beautiful she is?"

"Because that stupid chit told me to."

"How dare you call Miss Peabody stupid!"

"Not her, Miss Spalding, the elder one. And never mind, we can argue about this later. You must come back to England and marry Emily before Peabody takes it in his head to wed her to Steiker."

"Steiker?!"

"Aye."

"She can't wed him!" the marquis said, alarmed. "But how do we get back to England? We don't have enough money for one fare across the Channel."

Reed had never felt so blue-devilled in his life. He was tired, dirty and destitute. And he knew exactly whom to blame. A certain russet-haired, dark-eyed Miss Vivian Spalding. If she had not interfered, if she had not possessed that habit of poking her nose into what didn't concern her, none of this would have happened.

After an hour of walking, the two men came to a small posting house.

"Let's go in," the marquis said.

Reed hesitated. "I've had enough of French inns."

Ludwin nodded. "Perhaps you're right to be cautious. I'll go in, and if I don't come out in ten minutes, you come after me."

"Very well."

Since he had no timepiece, Reed counted off the seconds. He had just reached 852 when Ludwin emerged from the inn, wearing a grin and carrying a flask.

"Haven't you drunk enough wine?" Reed asked.

"They would foist it on me."

"They?"

"The men."

"Frenchmen being hospitable to an Englishman? There has to be a reason."

"Oh, there's a reason, Reed. And I have devised a way to get back to England. Come and see."

He led a bewildered Reed into the inn, where a group of men were gathered round a billiard table.

"*Voila*," the marquis said with a flourish.

Reed's head swivelled in the direction of the table and then back at the marquis. "Billiards? How is a billiard table going to help us?"

Ludwin took him of to the side. "We need money to get across the Channel," he told Reed. "And am I or am I not the best billiard player in London?"

"You are... but..." Reed broke off. "Can you mean wagering?"

"I know your objections to wagering, but our situation is desperate, and I assure you it shan't be that bad."

Reed remained silent.

"We can't walk back to England. We'll need horses to get us to the coast. Besides, I already told them we would wager with them."

"We don't have any money to wager with," Reed reminded him in a harsh whisper.

"We won't need it, because I shall win," the marquis said airily.

For two pins Reed would have told him exactly what he thought of such a scheme. Gaming had been ruin of his father, but the circumstances, he had to admit, were different now and quite desperate. Neither he nor Ludwin had a sou between them. They would need funds. He tried not to think of what might be in store for them were Ludwin to lose and the Frenchmen to discover that their pockets were completely to let.

"Very well."

The marquis clapped him on the shoulder. "That's the spirit."

"You had better win. And not a word of this to anyone once we have returned to London."

Having deduced from the conversation that the arrangements between the Englishmen had been made, the Frenchmen approached, pushing forward the best of their players.

"Marcel is his name," Ludwin said, as they took turns practising on the billiard table. "Pity I don't have my own stick."

"The next time you fall into a drunken stupor you must remember to bring it," Reed said acidly.

He was busy collecting the slips of paper on which the Frenchmen had placed their bets. Marcel certainly commanded the support of his friends.

He tucked the papers into his pocket where his purse had once lain, accepted a glass of wine that was thrust upon him by a hospitable onlooker, and watched as the match commenced.

Nigel, exuding confidence from every pore, had the advantage of shooting first. His cocky grin irritated Reed beyond belief. But that irritation ended when he made his first mistake and the ball slipped off the side of a cushion.

"Blast!"

Marcel, chalking his cue, wore a grin nearly as broad as the marquis's, and he was uncanny in his accuracy as the game lengthened.

Reed would not have thought it possible, but the Frenchman was even better than Ludwin, an opinion that all the others in the room held, judging by the roars of approval which swept the inn.

Reed wiped away the perspiration dotting his forehead.

"Miss, blast you, *miss*," the marquis could be heard to mutter as he chewed on his lower lip.

Someone in heaven must have been listening, for Marcel, lining up his shot, misjudged the distance. The miscue cost him dearly, as Nigel took the first game.

"Bravo!" Reed pounded his friend on the back, then drew the wagering slips from his pocket. "We shall have enough to go back to England.

Marcel scowled and said something in French to the innkeeper, who hurried over.

"Marcel wishes a rematch."

"A rematch? Out of the question."

When this response was relayed to Marcel, he came forward with a group of his friends, all carrying cue sticks. The marquis retreated.

"I say, Reed, perhaps we ought to give the chap a rematch. What say you?"

"What if he wins?"

"If we don't give him a rematch, there might not be any of us left," the marquis pointed out.

Reed eyed the muttering crowd. He loved a good mill, but this was folly.

"All right, but if he loses, that is it. We won't play him again," he said to the innkeeper.

"One more chance is all he wants," the innkeeper agreed.

The same wagers were made, and the marquis took up the cue stick once again. Marcel, given a chance to redeem himself in the eyes of his fellow Frenchmen, was not grinning this time. Indeed, his eyes were deadly serious.

Reed felt a sinking sensation in his stomach, as Ludwin had to scurry after one well-placed shot after another. Marcel teased and toyed his way through the match, and the marquis, not used to this tactic, found himself shooting wildly.

"Think, man, think!" Reed called out his encouragement.

Ludwin pursed his lips and rammed a ball off the cushion. It came up inches short of where he wanted it. Marcel, grinning broadly now, brought the match to a merciful conclusion.

Cheers rocked the little inn. Marcel was hugged in an excess of Gallic fervour, pounded on the back, and toasted. The emotion spilled over onto the marquis, who was saluted as a valiant foe, and Reed, who had no choice but to return the wagering slips with a smile.

"Now, I know why I don't like wagering," he complained to Ludwin later as the boisterous crowd swelled about them.

"Look at it this way, Lucian," the marquis said. "We never had the money in the first place. So we haven't lost anything."

"And we haven't gained anything, either."

"Yes, we have," the marquis said, grinning as the innkeeper set a bottle of claret down in front of them along with a roast chicken and a wedge of cheese. "Our lunch, which we could not afford otherwise."

"But we still haven't found our way to Dieppe."

"Dieppe?" the innkeeper, busy filling glasses of wine, paused and looked at them. "Are you on your way to Dieppe?"

"Yes. Our horses went lame," the marquis said.

"Then you are in luck. Marcel is on his way with his wagon. He'll take you there!"

Marcel, when informed that his valiant opponent and friend were in need of transport to Dieppe, was only too happy to provide this service.

The marquis grinned again. "See, Lucian? Maybe it is a good thing I lost this match!"

AT FIRST REED HAD THOUGHT it a mistake to accept Marcel's transport to Dieppe. The Frenchman appeared to have any number of stops to make on the way, each apparently entailing the greeting of family and the consumption of a bottle of wine. Long before they reached Dieppe, Marcel was thoroughly foxed.

This might have been a problem, except that, being thus foxed, he was encouraged to lie down in the back. The marquis took over the reins, fighting with Reed for that honour.

"I am the better driver," Ludwin asserted.

"I am a member of the Four Horse Club, too," Reed reminded him, not looking forward to sharing the back of the wagon with a drunken Frenchman.

"Yes, so you are, but I outrank you," the marquis said. "Don't worry, Lucian. You shan't suffer long. We shall make Dieppe by nightfall."

Ludwin was not far off the mark, for they did make Dieppe by eight that evening and parted company with Marcel. Unfortunately, they were not able to board the ferry to take them across the Channel, for the ferry had been twice delayed and a veritable horde of passengers waited who must board first.

"We shall just have to wait our turn," Ludwin said equably, "Besides, we have a problem that neither of us anticipated."

"Which is?" Reed asked irritably, his mood rendered testy by his being obliged to cool his heels while everyone else in Christendom boarded the ferry.

"How shall we pay for passage across? We still don't have a sou between us."

"Blast!" Reed had forgot the condition of their purses. But somehow they must reach England. He was heartily sick of France and everything to do with the country, including its snoring natives. As he stood wondering what Banbury Tale he could use to wrangle passage aboard he heard his name called.

He turned and nearly went ashen with shock.

"Good God, it is you!" Vivian Spalding declared and burst into laughter.

Vivian tried in vain to subdue her amusement, but it was really too absurd. There stood the usually elegant Reed with his handsome face now smudged with dirt, his neckcloth torn and not even a coat on his back. He looked tired and angry, and she couldn't help laughing again.

Reed had borne enough indignities during the past week to last a lifetime. This whole wretched trip to France had been Vivian's fault, and now she had the gall to stand there, laughing at him! It was the final straw.

Without thinking, he reached one lanky arm out and pulled her against him.

"Mr. Reed!" she exclaimed.

She got no further as his mouth descended on hers, silencing the laughter once and for all.

CHAPTER FIFTEEN

THE MOMENT REED'S LIPS touched hers, Vivian's laughter ceased. But he did not stop kissing her. Her mouth was incredibly sweet, her body so pleasantly soft against his. He sighed and kissed her again. It was simply not done, to be bussing any female in so public a place as a ferry crossing, but he did not care. He could feel the racing of her heart. Or was it his own heart that raced?

On the receiving end of Reed's kiss, Vivian felt her senses swirling in so dizzying a fashion that anyone would think she were drowning. She was acutely conscious of the lean, hard masculine arms holding her. It felt so right to return his kiss with all the ardour she possessed. She felt perfectly at home in his embrace.

Someone cleared his throat. "I say, Reed."

Breathlessly, Vivian pulled away from Reed. Her face flushed as she became aware of the marquis watching them.

"My lord, I didn't know you were there."

"Apparently not," Ludwin said with an engaging grin.

"More to the point, what are *you* doing here?" Reed asked thickly, wishing that Ludwin hadn't interfered just then. At long last he knew how to handle Miss Spalding: kiss her senseless.

"Crossing the Channel on the ferry," Vivian said now, drawing her cloak over her shoulders.

"Where is your sister?"

"Rory did not care to accompany me on this trip."

"Did she not?" Reed crossed his arms on his chest. "You may pitch your gammon at some other fool, Miss Spalding, but I have cut my wisdoms. What game are you playing at?"

"No game, Mr. Reed, I assure you."

"Where is Trawley? Does he know that you're racketing about like this?"

"No. He is not here, either."

"Do you have a maid with you?"

Vivian expelled a breath. "Good gracious, Reed, are you a paperskull? I am travelling alone."

"Why?"

"You have no right to interrogate me." *Or kiss me either,* she thought, as a part of her yearned for another of those soul-searing kisses. "You're not my guardian or my husband."

What had possessed her to say *husband?* Of course he wasn't her husband.

"No, that privilege falls to Trawley, doesn't it?"

"Trawley?" Just in time she remembered that no one as yet knew that she had jilted Trawley. How vexatious this all was. She had crossed to Dieppe and taken a night in a nearby inn, where she pondered her future in France. Her funds had nearly been depleted when she chanced onto a card-game in the coffeeroom. Her father's excellent tutelage concerning the principles of whist had led to refilling her coffers. She had won enough from her fellow travellers to pay for her passage to America. She intended to cross back to England and stay incognito until she could find a ship and book passage on it. Instead, whom must she encounter but Lucian Reed!

She smiled involuntarily at him now; his tall figure in no way resembled his usual sartorial splendour. If only Miss Long could see him.

"What is so amusing?" Reed asked, his lips lifting in an unconscious smile of his own.

"You are in that dirty rig with your hair askew and your cravat untied."

"Is it?" He reached automatically for his throat. "So it is."

"You look most unlike your usual self, Mr. Reed. You're acting most unlike your usual self, too."

"And you look and act quite like your usual hard-headed self, Miss Spalding. Now, do credit me with some wits and tell me what you are doing here, if you please?"

"I am returning to America."

"By way of France?" Ludwin asked.

"It sounds very strange, but I booked passage on the *Merriman* with a Captain Gouge and went to Bristol to board the ship, but it had left last week. It turned out that Gouge was a scoundrel and had been turned off the ship. He had taken my money and left me without passage to America."

"Why did you want to go to America?" Reed asked, his gaze deep and penetrating.

"Because of Trawley and Rory. They are in love, but since he is supposedly betrothed to me, there is no way he would jilt me and marry her. But if *I* jilted *him* and returned to America, then he could marry her."

"Did he know of this hen-witted plan?" Reed asked.

Her soft curls fell vigorously about her shoulders as she shook her head. "Of course not. Then the jilting would not come as a shock. I left a note behind for him."

"But how did you come to be in Dieppe?"

"Well, I was at sixes and sevens since the boat to America would sail on Tuesday. I couldn't go back to Trawle."

"Why not?"

"Because then the ensuing scandal might compel Trawley to do the honourable thing and marry me, and that wasn't what I wanted. I didn't have enough money to stay in Bristol an entire week. But I did have enough to cross the Channel, so I did."

"And now you are returning. Why?"

Vivian hesitated. She knew how set he was against gambling of any sort. Trawley had told her about Reed's father, the gamester who had lost the family home. He was bound to think the worst of her if he knew that she had spent her time at the French inn gambling.

"My French is abominable. So I decided it was best to return to England. I shall stay hidden until I can catch a ship to America."

"My dear Miss Spalding. A young lady cannot stay hidden away by herself."

"Why not? No one has seen fit to lay a hand on my person except you."

Recalled in this fashion to the searing kisses they had shared, Reed merely looked black.

"And now what are you doing here, sir?" she asked, turning the question back on him.

He glared at her. "I am doing a favour for you."

"For me? Surely you jest."

"I am assisting Cupid in the matter of Miss Peabody and Ludwin," he said scorchingly. "You don't know the shifts I've been put to. Peabody had me practically leg-shackled to his daughter when I left England."

"Didn't she turn you down?"

A trace of hauteur came into his blue eyes as he lifted his chin. "No, Miss Spalding, she did not."

"How strange."

"There are some ladies who consider me one of the prizes of the Marriage Mart!" he said, much stung.

"Would they still think that if they could see you now in all your dirt?" she asked.

"Oh, a good hit indeed," Ludwin interjected. "Miss Spalding's right, Reed. We look like a pair of ramshackle creatures ourselves."

"I am very well aware of the deprivations I have suffered trying to find you, Ludwin," Reed said frigidly, feeling hot, bothered and most unlike his usual cool, fashionable self. Why was it taking so long to board the ferry?

As though in answer to his unspoken question, a loud voice began to speak to the crowd in rapid-fire French. Reed's understanding of the language was poor at best, but he had no difficulty understanding the groan that greeted the announcement.

"I am going closer to see what has happened," Vivian said.

Before either man could say a word, she had slipped into the thick of the crowd.

"Now where the devil is she? Nigel, help me! We must follow and keep her out of mischief."

The marquis and Reed plunged into the crowd, which was surging every which way. Twice Reed had to stop because he could not push his way through. His irritation with Vivian had turned to fear. The danger of being trampled in a crowd of this size was real indeed.

"In a hurry, are you?" A bearded man turned to face Reed. He was French and spoke halting English.

"*Excusez-moi.* I was just trying to hear what had happened."

"There's no ferry tonight. Bad weather on the Channel. The crossing has been cancelled for tonight and probably tomorrow."

Reed swore.

"In a hurry to get home, are you?"

"That we are," Reed agreed. He scanned the crowd, searching for Vivian.

"Lost someone?" the bearded man asked.

"We are travelling with a lady," Ludwin explained. "She's an American, about this tall," he held up his hand to his shoulder. "Copper-coloured hair. Ah," he paused as his gaze finally fell on Vivian. "I see her."

The bearded man looked in direction of Vivian.

"Is it that *jolie fille*?" he asked.

"Yes," Reed said.

"She's a witch, is what she is," the man said. "Don't be fooled by her innocent face. Take it from one who has learned that the hard way," he added, and elbowed his way out of the crowd.

"What a peculiar man," Ludwin said to Reed. "Was he talking about Miss Spalding?"

"So it would seem. But she can't be acquainted with the likes of him, can she?"

"We must ask her," Reed said as he pushed his way towards Vivian.

She greeted him with relief. "Oh, Reed, they've cancelled the crossing."

"Yes, so I heard."

"Now what do we do, Reed?" Ludwin demanded. "We don't have any money for a posting house."

Vivian's eyebrows lifted. "You don't?"

"We were robbed in France," Reed explained. "Made our way to Dieppe and hoped to secure passage across."

"Exactly how much money do you have?"

"Nothing."

Ludwin cleared his throat. "How much money do you have, Miss Spalding?"

"Ludwin! Nothing would induce us to take funds from Miss Spalding."

"Oh? No, of course not."

"Don't be absurd. You are welcome to whatever funds I have, which will be enough to secure us a room for the night at a posting house and to cover the crossing to Dover for you both. But you must promise that once in England neither of you will reveal to Trawley or Rory or Lord Atwater where I am. And that you will repay me the funds you borrow, since I shall need every penny for my passage to America."

"We promise," the marquis said.

Just then the bearded fellow moved through the crowd.

"Do you know that man?" Reed asked. "Fellow with the beard."

Vivian instantly recognized the man as one of the card-players who had lost to her at the inn.

"Do you know him?" Reed repeated.

"No, I do not," Vivian lied.

Reed stiffened. He heard the tremor in her voice. She must be lying; he knew it instinctively. Yet why? The fellow was obviously not of the Quality. What kind of connexion could he have with Vivian? He turned his thoughts to Vivian's previous tale of misfortune at the hands of the captain. If she had been nearly penniless, how had she got enough money to pay her passage back to England, and his and Ludwin's and the night's stay in a posting house?

Unless... had she granted certain favours to the bearded man and others of his ilk as a way of getting money?

No! Reprehensible idea! She was a lady. Surely, there was another way.

"Are you feeling quite the thing, Mr. Reed?" Vivian asked now. "You look quite green."

"I am perfectly stout."

"Don't be silly. To be pressed in a crowd this way is most distressing. I have heard it said that ginger settles the stomach," she said, digging into her reticule for a small sliver of gingerbread.

"My stomach needs no settling, Miss Spalding," he replied. "It is kind of you to offer us a room for the night and passage back. How came you by your money?" he asked quietly.

Nibbling on the bread herself, she began to choke. "I beg your pardon?"

"You told me that the captain had taken your money earlier, leaving you with very little to fly with. Nevertheless you secured passage to France, spent at least one night at a French inn and then arranged passage back to England, with enough left over to assist me and Ludwin. Did a miracle occur at the French inn?"

"Miracle? Hardly. Are you certain you don't want a piece of gingerbread?" She held it up to him.

He pushed her hand away.

"How did you get the money?" he asked.

She turned and put the gingerbread back into the pocket of her cape. "That is none of your affair, sir."

"Why won't you tell me?" he asked, touching her shoulder.

She was silent. Reed's kiss had stirred up such hope in her breast. She knew beforehand that she loved him. His kiss and the resulting passion within her had merely confirmed those feelings. But she also knew his opposition to gambling.

Reed's hand dropped from her shoulder. Her silence was answer enough.

"Come," the marquis urged. "Let's see about finding a room for the night."

But this task soon proved impossible. All the inns were full. Reed began to fret about a new problem: Miss Spalding's presence in their company might put her in a compromising position.

"In the event that we do find a room for the night, I think you should say that you are Ludwin's sister," he told her as they walked away from the last inn they had tried.

"Why on earth?"

"To be in the company of two men so late at night might be considered..."

"Oh, fiddle. Next you will be saying that I am compromised and that I had better marry one of you."

"It is to keep such a thing from happening that I am suggesting that you pretend to be Ludwin's sister."

"Well, it's a foolish idea. Don't you think so, my lord?" she demanded, turning to the marquis.

"Reed may be right," Ludwin said. "Not that you would enjoy being either of my sisters. Bran-faced brats, the pair of them. But it would protect your reputation."

Still arguing the point with her two friends, Vivian continued down the road. She found herself relying more than she wished on Reed's strong arm. Once she would have fallen if not for his quick move to hold her upright.

"You are tired," he said.

"No, not at all."

Before she could protest, he'd swung her into his arms to carry her.

"We must find some place where we can take shelter for the night," he told Ludwin.

"Aye. But where?"

"Put me down, Reed," she said drowsily.

"Be quiet, minx." He shifted her in his arms.

"I am too heavy."

"I am not such a weakling."

"Hush, I hear something," Ludwin said.

It was a carriage approaching.

"*Arrêtez-vous!*" Ludwin called out. The vehicle pulled to a stop.

"*Qu'est-ce que c'est?*" A woman's voice enquired.

"Would you help three English persons who have been stranded in your country?" Ludwin asked.

With the help of a lantern held by a groom, the Frenchwoman peered out of the carriage.

"What's that you say, stranded?" she asked in heavily accented but understandable English.

"Yes. The weather has turned foul over the Channel. No one can cross."

"*Mon Dieu!*" she exclaimed. "I was to pick up some English actors who are to perform tomorrow for my papa's birthday surprise. It is all arranged. And now you say the ferry has not arrived."

"Bad luck all round," Reed agreed. "We haven't been able to find a room for the night."

"And your friend is very tired."

"Yes. Ludwin's sister, actually," Reed said.

The Frenchwoman said nothing for a moment. "You are English."

"Yes, we are."

"Good. I suppose you have been to the plays of Mr. Shakespeare?"

"Time and again. Why?"

"Because I have an idea. I shall put the three of you up for the night at our house, in exchange for your agreeing to put on a small performance for my papa's pleasure."

"Performance? But we're not actors."

"But you have been to the theatre, *n'est-ce pas?* You could stage some little scenes of Mr. Shakespeare. I would hate to have Papa's birthday fête spoiled because the actors did not arrive. It is the perfect solution, *oui?*"

It was a solution, and though far from perfect, the only one that any of them could see.

"And I shall also pay you what I was going to pay the English actors."

"Very well," Reed said and handed Vivian into the carriage.

CHAPTER SIXTEEN

AS THE CURTAIN OF SLEEP lifted the next morning, Vivian felt a momentary confusion as to her whereabouts. This wasn't her room back in her Philadelphia home, nor was it Lord Atwater's huge four-poster in London. Trawle, perhaps? But no, the ceiling was painted an entirely different colour. She closed her eyes, hoping that would nudge her memory. *France.* Of course!

But this wasn't the short and narrow bed at the inn where she had spent a night, she realized as she rolled over. She yawned and stretched, feeling her limbs relax. Where was she? She remembered meeting Reed and Ludwin at the ferry crossing and trudging along with them after the ferry's cancellation, trying to find shelter. Dim memories of a carriage ride and someone speaking French to her came and went. No use. She must have fallen asleep.

She pushed the lace-trimmed coverlet off now and made her way towards the porcelain pitcher and basin in the corner of the room. As she finished her ablutions, a knock on the door sounded. A maid entered, carrying a breakfast tray.

"*Bonjour, mademoiselle,*" she said gaily.

"*Bonjour,*" Vivian replied.

Her French was very bad, and the maid's English proved nonexistent, but once the cover was lifted off the tray, no words were necessary. Vivian eagerly returned to bed, thumped two pillows and placed them behind her and feasted on fresh country eggs, flaky croissants and a steaming cup of chocolate that tickled her nose. How on earth had Reed found these accommodations? she wondered after she had finished eating and was dressing herself. The maid had shaken the wrinkles out of the clothes in her travel bag and had laid them out on a chair. And *where* on earth were the two gentlemen?

Before she had an opportunity for further questions, another knock sounded on her door and a smiling Frenchwoman appeared, wearing a blue-sprigged cotton dress.

"You are awake," she said.

"Yes," Vivian replied, glad that the other woman spoke English. "Thank you so much for your hospitality."

"De rien," the woman replied. "It is I who am thankful to you for helping me with my little problem."

"Oh?" Vivian felt herself on uncertain ground. What "little problem" could the Frenchwoman be alluding to?

In due course she learned that the Frenchwoman's name was Yvette LeGrande. "Your brother and friend have told me all about you, Lady Vivian."

"They have?" Vivian wondered just what type of tale had been spun by her *brother* and friend.

Yvette's blue eyes danced. "They are so handsome, both of them. You are lucky to have one for a brother and the other for a lover."

Vivian choked. "Lover!" Had Reed told her that? "Miss LeGrande."

The Frenchwoman smiled archly. "Perhaps I am premature. He is not your lover yet. But he is certain to be, judging by his manner with you. The way he laid you on the bed so tenderly last night, carrying you in himself and refusing my servant's offer of assistance."

"Did he?" Vivian put a hand to her throat, recalling now how Reed had carried her fatigued body on the road. "I don't remember everything."

"You were very tired. You must be eager to see him."

"Yes, and my brother, of course."

Yvette skipped to the window and gestured to Vivian to join her.

"*Voilà,*" she exclaimed.

Vivian glanced out of the window and inhaled a quick breath. Down below on the garden terrace, Reed and Ludwin were fighting furiously with swords. And judging by the sound of the blows each exchanged they were deathly serious about it.

"Have they gone mad!" she exclaimed. "I must stop them."

"Lady Vivian!" Yvette called after her, but Vivian paid no attention. What on earth was possessing Reed and Ludwin to fight with each other? It couldn't be a duel, could it? What would they fight over? Not her, surely?

With her thoughts revolving like a Catherine wheel she flew down the stairs and out into the garden.

"Stop it! Stop it!" she exclaimed, charging towards the two men.

Neither man appeared to hear her, but Ludwin, who had been about to deliver the fatal blow, certainly felt her as she jumped on his back and pulled at his right arm.

"Good Jupiter!" he exclaimed, falling to one knee from the weight of her leap.

Reed grinned from ear to ear. "Good morning, Miss Spalding. I trust you slept well."

"Slept well?" She stared at him. His hair gleamed in the sunlight. With his coat off and sword in hand he looked as dashing as a pirate. "How can you speak of sleeping, when you and Ludwin are fighting in this reprehensible fashion."

"I see Yvette hasn't explained things to you."

Vivian frowned as she disengaged herself from Ludwin's back. "All she said was that she had a little problem that we were to help her with."

"Lady Vivian!" The Frenchwoman was hurrying now across the garden steps. "There you are." She smiled at the two men. "How is your rehearsal progressing, gentlemen?"

"Tolerably well," Ludwin replied. "Although Reed must learn to pull back his blows or there will be none of me left."

"Rehearsal?" Vivian looked from one face to another.

"Miss LeGrande had need of a trio of English actors who didn't make it across the Channel last night," Reed explained. "In exchange for the beds we slept in and the excellent meals she furnished we have agreed to put on a performance at her father's birthday fête."

"Performance? Acting?"

"And I will pay you ten gold pieces," Yvette added.

"Yes, mustn't forget the ten gold pieces," Reed replied. "What you perceived as a real battle between your brother and myself was merely acting: Hamlet and Laertes' fight to the finish."

"Ah, bon!" Yvette clapped her hands. "That is one of Papa's favourites. Now, you must excuse me. I'm sure you will want to rehearse as well, Lady Vivian. And I must see to the preparations for the fête."

"I will need to rehearse?" Vivian asked after Yvette had left her with the two men.

"You cannot fight shy of helping us with this project, Miss Spalding," Reed said, sheathing his sword. "Particularly since you enjoyed the benefits of the bed and a morning meal."

"Well, no," she said, feeling duty-bound to help however she could. "But I have never acted before in my life. Have either of you?"

Here Ludwin manfully confessed that he had once or twice performed in an amateur theatrical at the urging of his sisters and mother.

"Then as you are the only one of us with experience treading the boards, you must be our director," Reed said, clapping him on the shoulder. "It was Ludwin's idea to stage the sword fight in *Hamlet*," he told Vivian. "Since we both fence, there's the advantage that if we forget our lines the audience won't notice."

"It must have been true enough to life, to compel you to fly down from your bedchamber and jump on my back," Ludwin said to Vivian.

"Sisterly concern for the welfare of her brother," Reed quipped.

"Just so," Vivian agreed, not wanting to meet his eye.

"Then why was it that you grabbed *my* arm, Miss Spalding?" Ludwin asked curiously.

Taken aback by the question, Vivian searched her mind for a reason which would satisfy both grinning gentlemen. "You were the one nearest to me," she said lamely. "And just how long a performance are we slated for?" she asked, turning the topic.

"An hour. That shan't be too difficult," the marquis said with aplomb. "And now, as director, I think perhaps you and Reed should do that balcony scene from *Romeo and Juliet*."

"Oh you do, do you?" Reed said.

"Impossible!" Vivian concurred.

"Oh, come now, you two. It's quite a famous scene and that means you won't have to fret over the lines."

"Then why don't you put yourself in the scene?" Reed asked.

"Because Vivian is supposed to be *my* sister. It won't wash. Besides, you and she share some feeling for each other," he said slyly, "and that will come out in the performance."

"My lord, you mistake the matter," Vivian said.

"Oh, have I?" he asked blandly.

"Miss Spalding is right."

"Well, never mind my mistake. Just do the thing, will you? Then we will only need another twenty minutes or so, which we can easily fill with a few of Shakespeare's sonnets."

"Miss Spalding might like to try another scene. What think you of the part of Kate in *The Taming of the Shrew?* Or the sleep-walking Lady MacBeth?" Reed asked.

Vivian laughed in spite of herself. "You are incorrigible, sir."

"You do see we have to put the best face possible on our meagre talents," Reed coaxed.

"Very well, I will be Juliet."

"There are some copies of Shakespeare's Quartos in the library to refresh your memory."

"And perhaps you could go through the sonnets," Ludwin added. "See which ones you might care to recite and mark some others for us."

ACQUIESCING TO THIS suggestion, Vivian spent the next hour in the LeGrande library, leafing through the Quartos. Ensconced in a leather armchair with a tray of refreshments in front of her, she was pleasantly surprised to find the time passing quickly. Yvette herself peeked in to find out how the matter of the performance was progressing.

"Very well," Vivian replied, glad of the break in her reading. "And the arrangements for the fête, mademoiselle?"

Yvette rolled her eyes ceilingward. "I am grateful that Papa's birthday comes but once a year. I have spent the last hour separating the two chefs in the kitchen. I know Henri is angry because he is the usual chef, but for such a big party he needs Gaston's help. He will not admit it, however."

"A good deal of fuss and botheration."

"*Oui...*" Yvette picked up a brass paperweight from the desk. "Your brother, Lady Vivian, is he married?"

"Not yet. But he has a particular friend back in London," she made haste to say.

Yvette took this answer philosophically. "*Tant pis.* He is very handsome." She pushed herself out of the leather armchair. "Now, I shall return to the kitchen and find out what other disasters await."

"There is one other thing, mademoiselle. We didn't bring costumes with us."

"*Je le sais.* But I have trunks filled with old clothes in the attic. Perhaps you could improvise?"

After choosing the sonnets that she thought would do the trick, Vivian climbed the attic stairs to find the trunks of old clothes. The room was dusty and crowded, and she began sneezing as soon as she entered.

She was still sneezing when Ludwin and Reed found her there.

"I do hope you haven't caught a chill," Reed said, a look of concern in his blue eyes. "The wind last night was cold."

"It's just the dust, sir."

"Can't be sure of that," he said, laying a hand on her forehead. "No fever."

"I am perfectly stout, I assure you." She moved quickly away from the unexpected touch of his hand on her bare skin.

"You do look a little flushed," Ludwin observed.

"I am fine," she said with a touch of asperity. "And if I am sneezing, it's only because of the dust here as I go through the trunks looking for costumes for our performance."

"No costumes will be necessary for our Hamlet and Laertes," Reed said.

"Be sensible, Lucian. Do you plan to use your good shirt and ruin it? Remember that we are going to have red dye for blood."

"I'd forgot," Reed said. He glanced at the trunk. "Let's see what's in that old thing, shall we?"

The next twenty minutes passed as the two gentlemen tried on shirts they unearthed from the trunk. Vivian averted her eyes as they stripped to the waist before donning the new shirts. She tried not to think about Reed standing only a few feet from her, bare chested, as he struggled into one garment and then another. Each proved to be too narrow at the shoulders.

"Can't fence in this," he said, practising a lunge and ripping a sleeve.

Vivian tried not to notice the bulging muscle of his arm which showed through the ruined shirt. If anyone knew that she had stayed in the same room while two men stripped to their waists, she would not have a shred of reputation left.

But then she doubted she'd had a shred of reputation left since the moment she had touched French soil. Surprisingly, she was not overly concerned. Besides, she was going back to America, wasn't she?

Finally, in the very last trunk, Ludwin found two shirts that would do the trick.

"That takes care of Hamlet and Laertes. Now for Romeo."

"This will do for Romeo as well," Reed protested.

"It certainly will not. You'll have blood on it," Ludwin pointed out.

"What about this, sir?" Vivian asked, pulling out a very plain white shirt that looked to be something one about to enter orders might wear.

"Rather drab," Reed said speculatively.

"It's not supposed to be the height of fashion," Ludwin objected with a sigh. "Try it on."

Vivian averted her eyes yet again, and Reed replied that the shirt would do.

"But I shall wear my own trousers."

"Thank heaven for that," Vivian murmured to herself.

"And what of Juliet? Have you found anything, Miss Spalding?" Ludwin asked.

"I have these three dresses which I shall try on in my bedchamber," she said.

"Let's see. Hold them up in front of you," Reed ordered.

She obeyed, holding up first a brown-and-gold dress, then a white muslin, and finally a pink one.

"The white or the brown-and-gold," he said decisively. "Pink would not do you justice."

Vivian smiled. "You have broken your vow, sir."

"Vow?" He cocked his head at her.

"About never commenting on my dress."

He chuckled. "But I wasn't commenting on your dress, only on your costume as Juliet. There is a world of difference."

"Go down and change, Miss Spalding," Ludwin urged. "We'll meet you outside in the garden to rehearse."

"Rehearse?" She looked puzzled.

"Your scene with Lucian. You can't just do the performance this evening without a rehearsal, can you?"

She had not anticipated that she would need to rehearse the love scene as well as perform it.

"In thirty minutes?" Ludwin asked.

"Agreed."

Back in her bedchamber Vivian stripped off her day dress and pulled on the white muslin. It made her look as young as Rory, she realized. Juliet was supposed to be very young. The brown-and-gold was a better choice if she wanted to look like herself; the earth tones brought out the colour of her hair and eyes. But she wasn't playing herself. She was playing Juliet.

"'BUT, SOFT! WHAT LIGHT through yonder window breaks? It is the east, and Juliet is the sun! Arise, fair sun, and kill the envious moon....'"

Feeling self-conscious as he directed his eyes up towards Vivian waiting on the balcony, Reed soon forgot the next words.

"Blast and botheration!"

"'Who is already sick and pale with grief,'" Ludwin prompted, but the mood had been broken and Reed, shaking his head, sat down on the stone wall by the terrace.

"I shall be sick and pale with grief if I attempt to play Romeo tonight," Reed said acidly.

The marquis paid him no mind. "Just study your lines," he urged. "Perhaps we should practise your speech, Vivian," Ludwin called up to her, "while Reed memorizes his again."

Obligingly, Vivian launched into her first speech. Ludwin could not fault her for the words, which she uttered perfectly, but passion and meaning in those words were sorely absent. He had supposed that this would be the perfect scene for Reed and Vivian, but now he wasn't sure. Both seemed to be taking pains to keep whatever true feelings they had for each other under cover. As a director it was his task to bring those feelings out.

"How was that?" Vivian called down.

"I'm afraid you are a trifle stiff, wooden. Remember, you are supposed to be in love. One look at this man, Romeo, sets your heart aflame!"

"Really, my lord!" Vivian exclaimed.

"Oh, you know what I mean. We are play-acting, after all. It doesn't mean anything, really. But when you utter Mr. Shakespeare's words you are Juliet in love with her Romeo. The same goes for you, Reed." He turned to his friend. "You are reciting, not acting. Perhaps if you came down here, Vivian, and were closer at hand, it would be easier to play the scene."

Easier for whom? Reed wondered fifteen minutes later as he dutifully mouthed Mr. Shakespeare's words to Vivian. When she was far up on her balcony, the distance had been enough to blot out his emotion. But now she was so close that he could reach out and touch her, and he felt his control beginning to slip.

"Much better, Lucian!" Ludwin beamed. "I think you are getting the hang of this."

"Humph..."

"And now, Vivian, please begin again, from the middle of your part."

"'Thou know'st the mask of night is on my face Else would a maiden blush bepaint my cheek...'" Vivian said, feeling her own cheeks redden under Reed's intent eyes. Her voice faltered, trembled and her gaze fell. "I'm sorry; now I have forgot my words."

Ludwin stroked his chin. "Why don't we pause for a few minutes? I need to think of a way to stage this scene."

With relief Vivian buried her nose again in the pages of Mr. Shakespeare's Quarto, while a distracted Reed helped himself to a glass of lemonade that Yvette had brought out for them. Acting was thirsty work. He took a glass of lemonade to Vivian.

"Thank you," she said.

"I've never realized before that acting was hard work. Siddons and Kean have my heartfelt sympathies."

She laughed.

"Do you agree?"

"I suppose so," she said. "Though I've never seen those two actors you mention. In truth, I've only seen a few plays in Philadelphia and none at all in London."

"But Drury Lane is one of the top theatres," he said. "You must see a performance there."

"Perhaps on my next trip to England."

But when would that be? he wondered. He realized that she had spoken.

"I beg your pardon, I was wool-gathering."

"I merely asked if you needed to look over Mr. Shakespeare's words." She handed him the pages as she spoke.

"Thank you. I know the words well enough. It's just that they trip over my tongue each time I try to say them."

"I know the feeling," she agreed.

He smiled at her. "We are a hapless pair of lovers, are we not, Miss Spalding?" he asked quietly. "Mr. Shakespeare has written the words out and still we stumble over them. Why is that, do you suppose?"

"Perhaps because we are thinking too much, sir," she said, averting her eyes from his. "Perhaps we should just follow our hearts and feelings."

"You may be right," he said. "Shall we practise a little—just the two of us—without Ludwin smiling at us in that idiotish way of his?"

She smiled. "If you like."

"I should like it very much."

CHAPTER SEVENTEEN

THE EXTRA PRACTICE DID the trick. By the time the performance hour grew near Vivian was feeling much more confident about her role, and dressing like Juliet in the white muslin made her feel as giddy and youthful as any lady in love.

Ushering her guests towards the chairs on the terrace, Yvette smiled her encouragement from below. Ludwin and Reed waited near the stone wall. Their sword fight would open the night's performance. Vivian and Reed would follow with their balcony scene and then would come the concluding sonnets.

The fête had been a huge success, judging by the smiles that wreathed the faces of the guests. Yvette's father, a garrulous man of sixty, reminded her of Lord Atwater. He pumped her hand and told her how pleased he was that he could take in their performance.

"Attention!" Yvette clapped her hands for quiet. She made a short speech in French, gesturing towards Reed, Ludwin, and Vivian on the balcony, no doubt making introductions of the actors.

Then, with another short speech, Yvette withdrew, leaving Reed and Ludwin to enact the sword fight between Hamlet and Laertes. And if Vivian had not known it was acting, she would have thought the two men intent on killing each other. A few in the audience shrieked at the violent exchange of blows. The red dye staining Reed's shirt was excellently received and at least one susceptible female fainted.

Vivian joined the applause, smiling down at both Ludwin and Reed as they took their bows.

Do not just say the words, but feel them, she reminded herself as she gazed down at Reed, now wearing a fresh shirt and a very different expression on his face.

"'O Romeo, Romeo! wherefore art thou Romeo? Deny thy father and refuse thy name; Or, if thou wilt not, be but sworn my love, and I'll no longer be a Capulet.'"

Reed vaulted up towards the wooden trellis on the stone balcony.

"'Call me but love, and I'll be new baptized; Henceforth I never will be Romeo.'"

Good heavens, he's climbing the trellis! Vivian thought with alarm. This wasn't the way Ludwin had laid out the scene. But too late! She covered as best she could with her speech until Reed, hanging onto the swaying trellis, was just below her, an impetuous Romeo daring all for a kiss.

"'My true love's passion: therefore pardon me, And not impute this yielding to light love, Which the dark night hath so discovered.'"

She leaned over now to look at Reed. It was his turn to speak.

"Kiss me," he whispered.

"What?"

"I can't remember the blasted lines. Just kiss me."

She bent closer to him, and he seized her and pressed his lips to hers, kissing her with every ounce of strength he had until she felt perilously close to falling off the balcony.

She struggled free from him. His eyes glittered.

"'O, swear not by the moon,'" she stumbled on, "'lest that thy love prove likewise variable. Do not swear at all; Or, if thou wilt, swear by thy gracious self...'" She gave him no opportunity for further speech or kisses, racing through the rest of her lines as though the devil himself were after her. And perhaps he was.

"'Good night, good night! parting is such sweet sorrow That I shall say good night till it be morrow.'"

She lifted a hand to Romeo. Reed caught it in his and kissed it, then turned and bowed to the audience, who broke into vigorous applause.

"Do you think we were convincing, Miss Spalding?" he asked, making her a sweeping bow as he vaulted onto the balcony. He bussed her heartily, to the cheers of the onlookers below.

"You were certainly an audacious Romeo," she said, feeling uncharacteristically breathless.

"I know. The trellis was nearly the death of me. But hush. Ludwin is about to read a sonnet."

The marquis read two sonnets which constituted the end of the performance. Vivian and Reed made their way down the stairs and out into the garden, where they accepted the congratulations of Yvette and her father.

"The best fête I've had in years." Monsieur LeGrande said, throwing his hands out expansively. "And you—" he wagged a finger at Reed "—I nearly thought would kill yourself getting to Juliet."

"Yes," Ludwin said. "What possessed you, Lucian?"

Reed's eyes twinkled. "A man in love does crazy things, Monsieur le Directeur, don't you know that?"

"Before I forget, here are your ten gold pieces," Yvette said, laying a bag of coins in Ludwin's palm. "And I have some good news for you. One of my neighbours says his boatman is planning to cross the Channel tomorrow. If you wish to go across with him I can arrange it."

"Indeed! Did you hear, Reed?" the marquis asked, turning to his friends. "We can sail for England tomorrow. Aren't you pleased?"

A hollow feeling spread in the pit of Vivian's stomach. *Back to England. And then on to America.*

"I'm anxious to reach Emily's father," Ludwin said, a worried crease on his forehead.

"Of course you are," Reed said. "You and Miss Peabody must be reunited. Just as we all must get a good night's sleep. It's been a devilishly tiring day."

TIRED THOUGH SHE WAS, Vivian found sleep all but impossible. She tossed and turned on the comfortable bed. She was in love with Reed. She knew it now for certain. But he had never given her any sign of true partiality. They had, it was true, shared a few kisses, but she had a sinking feeling that he kissed her only to keep from throttling her. Besides, he considered her hoydenish and not the type of lady a gentleman like him would wish to marry.

Choking back a sob, she finally fell asleep near dawn. Scarcely hours later she was roused by the maid with the word that they must get to the crossing in time for the boat. She dressed in a desultory manner and said goodbye to Yvette and her father, hoping no one would mention how hagged she looked.

Ludwin and Reed were silent in the carriage, for which she was grateful. The groom set them down at Dieppe and found the neighbour's boatman.

"There will be a moment's wait," he reported back to them. "The boatman has promised to take over another passenger."

"I hope the boat is big enough," Reed said.

"It is. Never fear."

Another ten minutes passed before the delinquent passenger showed up. It was the bearded fellow who had warned Ludwin and Reed about Vivian. Seeing him again was no pleasure for Reed, who glanced out of the corner of his eye at Vivian.

Vivian, for her part, would have wished the bearded man to Jericho. Not only was he a poor card-player, he was prone to wail about his losses. And she hoped that he wouldn't divulge her secret to Reed. She knew well his dislike of gaming.

Luckily, the bearded fellow was in no mood for conversation and was suffering from too much wine. He held on to the side of the boat, groaning as it pitched first one way and then the other.

Once they reached England the bearded man went on his way. Reed took command and secured Vivian a room in an Eastbourne hotel.

"They know me here," he said, "so you shall be safe." He counted out five of the gold coins for her from the bag.

"That is too much," she protested. "You and Ludwin will need the money."

He gave a slight smile. "I'd forgot that your purse was so filled. The bearded fellow had a small part in that, am I not correct?"

The stricken look in her eyes was answer enough.

"You shall stay in your room and have all your meals sent up," he said quickly.

"I didn't return to England to become a prisoner," she protested.

"You are not the prisoner, ma'am. I am," Reed said roughly and took her into his arms.

He shouldn't keep kissing her, he told himself. It was entirely too habit-forming. But he couldn't help himself. She was a witch. The bearded fellow on the boat had been right. Had she favoured *him* with kisses like this? he wondered as his mouth roamed searchingly on hers.

Madness. She really shouldn't let him kiss her this way, Vivian thought, as once again she felt herself close to drowning. With a groan he broke the kiss.

"Stay within the room," he said thickly. "Don't go out."

He kissed her again, hard and swiftly and then left. Vivian sank gratefully onto the small bed in her room. So much had happened to her in so short a space of time that her weary nerves were strained to the breaking point. She was in love with Reed. That she knew full well. She stared down at the coins in her hand. They would see her comfortably until she could reach Bristol, from where she could sail Tuesday for Boston.

Tears swelled suddenly in her eyes. She didn't want to go back to Boston and Philadelphia; she wanted to stay in England. Because of Reed, she acknowledged with a heavy heart. But he thought her wild and independent, and if he ever knew that she had gambled while in France, that would be the end of anything between them.

LUDWIN DEPARTED immediately for London, leaving Reed to ride his horse without stop all the way to Trawle. The first person he saw when he dismounted was Rory, who came running up to him, waving. Trawley trailed behind her, looking like a mooncalf. So Vivian had been right about them.

"Reed? What the devil are you doing here?"

"Actually, George, you will never believe it if I told you the truth."

"Whose clothes do you have on?"

"A Frenchman's, I believe."

"Really? Is it a new fashion?"

Reed stared at him. "Fashion? Don't be daft, man. I'm dirty and tired, and you talk to me about fashion!"

"Lucian, how would it sit, if you were to tell me exactly what is going on?"

As Reed scrubbed himself in a tub, he related to the viscount the deprivations he had suffered in France, omitting only the part about Vivian and his acting.

"Peculiar business, your going after Ludwin, Reed."

"Had to, or else I'd be married to Miss Peabody."

"And where is Nigel?" Trawley asked, emptying another bucket of hot water on his friend.

"On his way to London and Miss Peabody."

"Didn't know you were that thick with the Peabody chit."

"I wasn't. I promised Miss Spalding."

"Ah, yes, Miss Spalding. Well, you can rest easy about her. She's bound for America."

"Is she?" Reed ran a bar of soap down his arm.

"Jilted me a few days ago."

"You don't appear to be suffering from it," Reed said quietly.

The viscount laughed. "No, I'm not. It was a blow to my pride, but then Rory pointed out that now that Vivian was returned to America, she and I could wed."

"Married? You?"

Trawley smiled ruefully. "I know it sounds mad, Lucian. But with Rory I don't fight shy of the idea. She's young, I know, so we shan't marry right away. Perhaps a year of betrothal. But I know that I love her."

"Won't Miss Rory miss her sister?" Reed rose and towelled himself off.

"Yes, she will. Wish there could be a way of getting her back from America."

"Be careful what you wish, George. You may get it."

An hour later Reed paced in the bedchamber that Vivian had occupied at Trawle. The note she had left George was on the small dressing-table. In the sturdy wardrobe hung five of her dresses. He ran a finger over the folds of a red walking dress and felt a surge of longing.

"Ah, Lucian, there you are. We were becoming worried about you." Trawley spoke from the door. His quizzing glass dropped as he surveyed his friend. "I hope the clothes you borrowed from me were satisfactory."

"To be sure," Reed replied, scarcely glancing at the mirror. "They have restored me to a sense of myself."

"Tall, cool, handsome."

"And a bit of a fashionable fribble."

His friend was taken aback. "Lucian, by Jove, what has come over you?"

"I don't know," he replied, looking grim.

"You're not a fribble. Could a fribble rout the Patronesses? Hunt down Ludwin in France? Bet huge sums of money he didn't possess in a crowded inn in France?"

Reed chuckled. "Thank you, Trawley."

The viscount reached out a hand and smoothed the shoulder of the coat Reed wore.

"That coat is too narrow for your chest."

Reed dismissed his friend's comment with a careless wave.

"It doesn't matter."

Trawley recoiled as though struck. "It doesn't?"

"No, of course not." Reed met Trawley's sceptical eye. "Clothes, I have learned, do not make the person. It's what lies inside that counts."

"And who taught you this?" the viscount demanded.

"A lady."

One Vivian Spalding by name, who had swept into his life, pell-mell, hurtling him along with her. Life was never boring with her. And why the devil was he talking to Trawley when he cold be in Eastbourne with Vivian?

"Where are you going?" his friend asked as Reed headed for the door.

"I'm going to grant you your wish, George."

"What wish is that?"

"To bring Miss Spalding back from America."

VIVIAN STARED DOWN AT the remains of her tea-tray. She wished that she could go out of the room and stretch her legs. But she had promised Reed she would remain within closed doors.

A pity she had no books to read or pencil and paper to write with. Moodily she extracted a deck of cards from her reticule. At least she could pass the time playing Patience.

Would she ever see Reed again? Or Rory? She knew that her sister would soon be basking in the love of Lord Trawley and his mother. Rory's future was assured now that Vivian was out of the picture. It was what Vivian had wanted... but why did it make her feel so forlorn? Was it because her own future was still so very uncertain?

A knock on the door brought her out of her brown study. She crossed swiftly and laid one ear against the solid oak.

"Who is it?"

"Reed."

Swiftly she unlocked the door. "Reed!" she exclaimed, then stopped. This was not the dishevelled Reed who had kissed her into furious silence or had risked his neck climbing the trellis to her on the balcony. Here stood the tall exquisite who had always seemed to hold her at arm's length.

The sparkle in her dark eyes died away. Reed, who had held his arms out, ready to swing her up against him, let them fall now to his sides.

"You've changed your clothes," she said and immediately chastised herself for so inane a comment.

"I've changed into Trawley's clothes," he corrected. "They were clean."

"I envy you," she said.

"Not for long..." He held up a bag that she recognized as her own satchel.

"How?"

"I, er, pinched the clothing from your old room at Trawle."

"Reed! You mean you stole them?"

He looked abashed. "I suppose I did. But it wasn't really stealing because they belonged to you. I hope they will do."

"They are clean, and that's the main thing."

"After you change I shall meet you in the coffeeroom in an hour."

An hour was just sixty minutes, Vivian realized with alarm as she went to the basin and began to scrub herself.

Reed had brought her red walking dress and she wondered if he had chosen it with particular care, or if he had just seized the first thing that caught his eye.

Her ablutions completed, she stepped into the dress and struggled with the buttons on the back, fastening them finally after twisting herself this way and that.

She had washed her hair earlier in the day and drew a brush through the still damp curls. She was trying to get her coiffure into shape when someone knocked on the door.

"Mr. Reed is waiting, miss," came the voice of the innkeeper's wife.

She pinned a ribbon in her hair and opened the door.

"Oh, miss, how pretty you look," the woman beamed. "Mr. Reed has ordered the best dinner our kitchen can make." She chattered on as she escorted Vivian to the private parlour.

Reed rose when she entered, and she was aware once again of how tall and distinguished he was.

"That dress becomes you."

"Thank you. Fanchon's doing."

"No, yours." He gestured towards the laden table. "I'm famished. Shall we eat?"

Vivian fell in readily with this suggestion. Over a tray of sweetmeats he asked her once again how she had got the money she needed for her passage to England from France.

She stared down at her plate. "I thought we'd agreed that that was none of your concern, sir. How is Rory?" she asked, changing the topic.

"She seems in perfect health, enjoying herself, and has George firmly tied to her apron-strings."

Vivian laughed. "I'm glad."

"She misses you."

"And I, her."

"In fact George charged me with a mission. To bring you back from America."

"What a curious request. Why would he make it?"

"Because he knows that Rory would not be able to tolerate a separation from you for too long."

Vivian smiled sadly. "She has him."

"True. But she needs you as well."

Vivian put down her fork and took a quick swallow of the wine.

"I can't stay in England. The situation is impossible. You forget that if I stay I shall have to marry Trawley."

"Not if you married someone else."

"Such as?"

"Me."

Her heart turned over in her chest. "Don't be foolish, Reed. You don't wish to marry me. I am a hoydenish American. Your wife must be fashionable and beautiful."

He snapped his fingers. "That for fashion. And as for beauty—have you ever glanced in a mirror?"

She flushed. He had risen from his chair and towered over her.

"Marry me, Vivian, and you can stay in England."

"I know why you're offering for me. You think you compromised me in France with Ludwin."

"My dear Vivian, I'm offering for you because I have been driven to distraction by you since the day you arrived in London. I've battled the Patronesses for you, endured being robbed in France, and all for love of you."

"Love?" Vivian asked, a wild hope resurrected in her breast.

"I love you, Vivian," he said. "And now, having made you this offer, I must ask: how *did* you get the money for Ludwin's fare and my own?"

She turned away, as the hope which had been rekindled died aborning.

"You are very kind to make me an offer of marriage, sir," she said stiffly. "But I must decline your offer. We are too different."

He caught her wrist. "I talked to that bearded man on the ferry. He called you a witch."

She turned, fury staining both cheeks red. "Then if you already know the truth, why do you torture me this way? I know what you must think. There is nothing worse in your opinion than one such as me. But it was the only scheme I could think of. I needed the money. I was desperate. Hate me if you must."

He stared into her eyes, knowing that he should despise her but unable to.

"I cannot hate you," he said, lifting his hands helplessly. "Even if you had granted favours to the entire ship I would still love and want you for my wife."

"'Favours to the entire ship!'" She recoiled. "How dare you say such a thing?"

He felt confused, a familiar state when it came to Miss Spalding.

"By Jupiter, answer me straight out. How did you come by your extra funds?"

She lifted her chin. "I played whist, sir."

Reed stared at that pointed chin, then threw back his head and laughed.

"You played *whist?*" he gasped.

She eyed him carefully. "And not for chicken stakes."

"No, never that," he said, trying to stifle his laughter and failing.

"What is so funny?" she demanded.

"Nothing." He wiped his streaming eyes. "Everything. You. Me. Come here, you witch," he said and reached for her.

She thought she was used to his kisses and the way they could inflame her own senses, but this one was so thorough that she felt as though it would never stop. Nor did she want it to.

"Reed, are you feeling at all the thing?" she asked, later, seated comfortably in his lap with her head against his chest.

"I am feeling quite the thing," he replied, stroking the back of her neck.

"I gambled. And I know how you despise gamesters."

"I gambled, too."

She pulled away and searched his face. "When?"

"In France, when Ludwin found a billiard table. I wagered imaginary sums of money and won. Then I wagered the real thing and lost."

She stroked his cheek with a forefinger.

"But that wasn't the biggest wager I ever made."

"What was?" she asked, lifting her head towards his.

"The gamble I took when I fell in love with you, my dear Vivian. Do you love me?"

"I adore you," she said. "My fashionable Mr. Reed."

His arms tightened around her. "I shall not be called that for much longer. I fear my interest in fashion kept me occupied only until you, my love, entered my life. I vow I have more important things to concern me than the cut of my coat."

"Such as?"

"Such as whether to kiss you on your right ear or on your left."

He solved that problem by kissing her on each in turn. She sighed and nestled closer.

"I'll get a special licence, and we can be married at Trawle this week. I don't think George will mind. The quizzes will talk, but that is nothing new for us, is it?" His eyes smiled at her.

"Married, this week? My dear Lucian, how am I to have a wedding dress fashioned in only a week? Fanchon will have a fit. The most fashionable man in England cannot marry a dowd...." She protested until he finally silenced her the only way he knew. With a kiss.

THIS JULY, HARLEQUIN OFFERS YOU THE PERFECT SUMMER READ!

Sunsational

**EMMA DARCY
EMMA GOLDRICK
PENNY JORDAN
CAROLE MORTIMER**

From top authors of Harlequin Presents comes HARLEQUIN SUNSATIONAL, a four-stories-in-one book with 768 pages of romantic reading.

Written by such prolific Harlequin authors as Emma Darcy, Emma Goldrick, Penny Jordan and Carole Mortimer, HARLEQUIN SUNSATIONAL is the perfect summer companion to take along to the beach, cottage, on your dream destination or just for reading at home in the warm sunshine!

Don't miss this unique reading opportunity.

Available wherever Harlequin books are sold.

SUN

HARLEQUIN
Romance

This August, travel to Spain with the Harlequin Romance FIRST CLASS title #3143, SUMMER'S PRIDE by Angela Wells.

"There was a time when I would have given you everything I possessed for the pleasure of taking you to my bed and loving you...."

But since then, Merle's life had been turned upside down, and now it was clear that cynical, handsome Rico de Montilla felt only contempt toward her. So it was unfortunate that when she returned to Spain circumstances forced her to seek his help. How could she hope to convince him that she was not the mercenary, unfeeling woman he believed her to be?

If you missed June title #3128, THE JEWELS OF HELEN (Turkey) or July title #3136, FALSE IMPRESSIONS (Italy) and would like to order them, send your name, address, zip or postal code, along with a check or money order for $2.75 plus 75¢ postage and handling ($1.00 in Canada) for each book ordered, payable to Harlequin Reader Service, to:

In the U.S.
3010 Walden Ave.
P.O. Box 1325
Buffalo, NY 14269-1325

In Canada
P.O. Box 609
Fort Erie, Ontario
L2A 5X3

Please specify book title(s) with your order.
Canadian residents add applicable federal and provincial taxes.

JT-B8R

Back by Popular Demand

Janet Dailey
Americana

A romantic tour of America through fifty favorite Harlequin Presents, each set in a different state researched by Janet and her husband, Bill. A journey of a lifetime in one cherished collection.

In August, don't miss the exciting states featured in:

Title #13 — ILLINOIS
   The Lyon's Share

#14 — INDIANA
   The Indy Man

Available wherever Harlequin books are sold.

JD-AUG